SP

The scene looked lik e
none other he had n
corpses. It was as if an army had passed through and all that was left were dead horses. As if the defeated army had taken their dead away and vanished. Joby felt the hackles rise on the back of his neck.

The eeriness of it took him back to Shiloh and Vicksburg, and he could almost see the white smoke of battle lingering in the grasses when the cannons and the rifles had gone silent.

Maybe he should have killed Zeke and his gang before they ever had a court trial. Just shot them down like the dogs they were. But he hadn't been raised that way, and the army sure as hell wouldn't have condoned such an act of vengeance. But this was personal. His sister and his wife had both been violated. At least Do had, and he had no doubt that Zeke would take his savage hatred for Joby out on Felicia.

And laugh while he did it, Joby thought.

He had seen and heard that laugh before.

In that moment, Joby made a decision. He would hunt down the men who had kidnapped his wife and make them pay for what they had done to her and to his sister.

And, he would do it all by himself.

"I'm coming, Felicia," he said to himself, and it sounded in his ears like a prayer. But it was a vow.

A vow he meant to keep.

TEXAS DUST

Jory Sherman

TEXAS DUST

A Berkley Book / published by arrangement with the author

PRINTING HISTORY
Berkley edition / January 2004

Cover illustration by Jim Griffin.
Cover design by Jill Boltin.

For information address: The Berkley Publishing Group, a division of Penguin Group (USA) Inc., 375 Hudson Street, New York, New York 10014.

ISBN: 0-425-19430-2

BERKLEY®
Berkley Books are published by The Berkley Publishing Group, a division of Penguin Group (USA) Inc., 375 Hudson Street, New York, New York 10014.
BERKLEY and the "B" design are trademarks belonging to Penguin Group (USA) Inc.

PRINTED IN THE UNITED STATES OF AMERICA

10 9 8 7 6 5 4 3 2 1

1

The first man rode into the settlement town after dark, so no one got a good look at his face. He put up at Mrs. McKinney's Boarding House, "like he knew where to go," her husband Bill would say later. He also said, "My Lucy didn't smell no liquor on his breath, so she took him in."

That one gave Mrs. McKinney the name of Ezekiel Popper and she wrote it down in her lodging book. "You can call me Zeke," he said. "Or ZP."

Mrs. McKinney said, "I'll call you Mr. Popper, if you don't mind."

He paid her for a whole week of days and nights in hard coin. She had the boy, Bub Marshall, put up the man's horse. Bub said the sorrel gelding had three brands on it and one that looked like it had been burned over with a running iron.

Lucille McKinney said later that she should have listened to her daughter, Veronica. "Ronnie whispered to me when he showed up at our door not to take him in. She said he looked like a hard case. We needed the money, but I should have listened to Ronnie."

The other strangers came in singly, after that night, like the first one, in darkness, and not like they all came from the same place. The second man put up at Lou Marshall's Bed & Livery. Lou was Bub's brother but he and Bub didn't get along. Lou had the man sign his book, too, and the name put down was Peter Hayes and he said he'd "rode in from Shreve's Port over to Louisiana."

Richard Lee Richardson came riding in the next night and he put up at the livery, too, but acted like he didn't know Pete Hayes and said he hailed from Nacogdoches, which might or might not have been true.

The other two louts put up their tents at Ortega's Camp at the south edge of town. They didn't have to sign a register for that, but Pedro Ortega said the names given were Roy Botts and Frank Duggan. They told Ortega they rode up from New Orleans, but he didn't believe them. They also said they were *vaqueros,* and spoke some Spanish, but Ortega noticed their hands were smooth and had no calluses. Their faces were burned from being in the sun, and the skin was dark and peeling, giving their complexions a splotchy appearance. "They all looked like men who might have been in prison for a long time and had not seen no sunlight until maybe a week before they come here," Ortega said. "They looked like ex-convicts to me." He further noted that they wore their six-guns low and had thongs looped over the hammers. He took them to be gunslingers, but didn't say anything at the time.

Sheriff Tom Keller noticed that all the men wore heavy leather chaps, and he further noticed that those chaps had deep scars in them, so he was reluctant to believe that any of the strangers had ridden in from the east. "Them boys come from brush country," he said later. "Like they was riding through country what didn't belong to them, and didn't want to go through no towns until they got to Gilmet."

Keller also noticed the tied-down six-guns and that the

holsters rode low on their hips, so their hands didn't have to travel very far to make a quick draw. Nobody around those parts wore big, heavy six-guns and none wore them like these boys did. But he didn't have any "wanted's" on them in his office, so he was just hoping they'd pass on through in a few days. He figured there was nothing much to keep them in Gilmet.

At first, none of the men seemed connected to one another, but, one by one, they found their way to the small saloon on Third Street, the one owned by Burt Logan, who had gone bust as a farmer and saw a better way to make money. He called it a tavern and named it the Big Piney Tavern, but everybody in town called it what it was, a saloon, not to give it any fancy appellation, but to call it what it was.

Sheriff Keller called the Big Piney his second office because he spent more time there than he did in his own office. The jail was almost always empty anyway, and there was little call for sheriffing, but he had been duly elected and he wore a big six-gun on his hip and made sure people noticed him when he was making his rounds at night. He made his rounds short and quick so that he could spend time at the Big Piney, and that's when he first saw Zeke Popper and wondered who he was.

By the time all the drifters were in town, Logan's little tavern was near plumb full every night, and the strangers seemed friendly enough and bought a drink or two for Sheriff Keller and didn't seem afraid of him. Nor did they act like they were hiding anything. Except that Zeke Popper always sat at the last table, with his back to the wall, facing the bat-wing doors.

None of the men drank much in the Big Piney, but stayed to themselves. Hardly anyone noticed that they looked at each other now and then before a couple of them bought bottles and left the tavern. Then, one by one, the other three walked out of the saloon and disappeared into the night. Pedro Ortega said he saw them all together that last night, just on the edge of his camp, passing a bottle between them and talking so low he couldn't hear a word they said.

That last day in town, Roy Botts walked over to the First Federal Bank of Gilmet and asked the bank manager, Mr. Bertrand Loomis, if he knew of any land for sale thereabouts and Loomis told him where the land office was, even though it was in plain sight right across the street and only a blind man could miss it.

A half hour later, Zeke Popper came into the little bank and walked up to Veronica McKinney, Bill's daughter, and asked her to change a fifty-dollar bill. She recognized him as a boarder at her mother's house and smiled at him and he smiled back.

"You'll have to see Mr. Reynolds over there at the teller's window," she said.

"I was hopin' you could do it for me," he said.

"No, sir, you have to see Mr. Reynolds." She pointed to the teller's window and Popper walked over to it and put the bill on the counter.

Reynolds gave him four ten-dollar bills, and two fives, and he touched a hand to his battered, greasy hat and thanked Veronica, instead of the teller. Then he said something that Loomis overheard. "I'll be seein' you, Ronnie."

Loomis saw the startled look on Veronica's face when Popper called her by her nickname, as if he had known her a long time, instead of just a few days.

That afternoon, all of the strangers gathered at the Big Piney Tavern and bought drinks for those inside. Word spread, and soon the tavern was full, so full that no one noticed the strangers slipping out, one by one, until none of them was left. But the drinks kept flowing and even the sheriff was there for the free whiskey.

The next time anyone saw Popper and the others was when they all rode in and pulled up their horses outside the bank. One onlooker thought it was strange that all of the men wore black dusters. None had seen those dusters before and thought they might have been a kind of costume. All of the men were heavily armed.

The smiles they had worn on their faces earlier that day were gone. Instead, they appeared grim and hard, as if they were all bent on doing the devil's work. With their black dusters and black hats, they each bore the likeness of the Grim Reaper himself.

"They looked like a bunch of undertakers," one eyewitness said later. "Come to collect the dead."

The eyewitness was wrong. These men had come, not as undertakers, but as widow-makers. And the black dusters they wore were not mourning clothes, but the garb of cold-blooded executioners.

2

Lou Marshall saw the men enter the stables. He blinked his eyes to make out who they were. Before he could actually see their faces, he was looking at a pistol stuck square against his nose.

"What d'y'all want?" he asked, sounding stupid even to himself.

"We're takin' us an extra horse, son," Frank Duggan said, cocking the pistol snubbed up against Lou's nose.

"And saddle and bridle," Richard Lee added.

"We taken a liking to that bay mare you got in that last stall."

"That horse ain't for sale," Lou said. "It ain't mine to sell noways."

"We know that," another voice said, and when Lou looked beyond the barrel of the Colt, he saw the man who had spoken last. He had seen him at the Big Piney. He was the one they called ZP. Or Zeke.

"That's Miss Veronica's horse," Lou said.

"Now, ain't you the bright one," Popper said.

"Well, you ought not to take that mare thouten you get Miss Veronica's permission."

"I'm takin' that mare to Miss Veronica," Popper said. "So, you needn't worry youself none about that."

"Well, then, I reckon that would be all right," Lou said. "But, I really ought to have permission from her to let you take that mare."

Popper had run out of patience. He stepped up to Duggan and touched the pistol in his hand. "Put that away, Frank. Use the knife and cut this loudmouth's throat."

Duggan nodded and let the hammer back down before holstering his pistol. He drew his knife, a big-bladed bowie, with sharp edges on either side.

Lou's face turned ashen and beads of sweat broke out along the creases in his forehead. He started shaking his head, then dropped to his knees.

"Don't cut me," Lou begged. "Please. You don't need to cut me with no knife."

"I ain't goin' to cut you but once, pilgrim," Duggan said. "And it ain't goin' to hurt none."

"You—you mean to kill me," Lou said.

"Tell him why, Frank," Popper said.

Frank grinned and looked down at Lou. "We don't want nobody follerin' us, boy, so we're kind of leavin' a message behind."

"Please don't kill me," Lou pleaded.

"Get it over with, Frank," Popper said. "We ain't got all day."

Lou began to tremble. His lips moved, but no sound came out. He put his hands together as if to pray, and that's when Duggan grabbed his hair at the back of his head, pulled his head back, then slid the blade across Lou's throat, cutting deep with the sharp blade. Lou made a gurgling sound as blood gushed from his throat. The blood sprayed all around and Duggan pushed his head forward, knocking Lou down onto his face. Popper had stepped back so none of the blood splattered him. He and Duggan watched the blood pool up beneath Lou's slit neck while the others pulled the now-bridled bay mare out and saddled her quickly. It seemed that they had seen this before and Lou's death was not worth noting.

Duggan leaned down and wiped the blood from the blade of his knife on the back of Lou's shirt. The fallen man was still quivering, and one of his hands trembled. But, in seconds, all movement stopped and he lay still, face down in the straw and dirt and horse droppings.

The men led the mare out of the stables and mounted up without a backward glance at Lou Marshall as the flies began to swarm and drink the dead man's blood, not only on the ground, but on his gaping throat as well.

The men rode to the First Federal Bank, leading the bay mare, and only a few people were on the street, regarding them with curious expressions on their faces.

Two men, Botts and Duggan, stayed outside, holding Greeners at the ready, while Popper, Richardson and Hayes went inside. Those who witnessed this on the street were too dumbfounded to realize what was happening. They just stood there and gawked.

Richard Lee was the oldest of the bunch, but not their leader. He had salt-white specks in his black hair and puffy flesh under his cold, blue eyes. He walked right up to Mr. Loomis and put the barrel of his .44 Remington conversion in the man's gut. "You open that safe in your office real quick, Loomis, or your innards will feed the hogs tonight."

People in the bank wondered how Richardson knew the name of the bank manager, since none of the employees had ever seen the man before.

"The rest of you just keep your hands up where I can see 'em," Popper said, and people there, both customers and clerks, took him to be the leader. He was a burly man with thin scars on the bridge of his nose and on his cheekbones, a flabby neck, and small porcine eyes that sent chills up a man's spine at close range. His eyes seemed to be as black as anthracite coal, but they were actually brown, a dark brown, and the whites of his eyes were mottled with brown, as well, as if he carried some kind of disease or drank too much coffee, or smoked too many cigarettes.

Popper nodded to the head clerk, Mr. Elmer Reynolds, and that one began to clean out the cash drawers. He put the bills in a canvas bag and handed another one to Hayes, who took it into Mr. Loomis's office and handed it to Richardson.

Loomis opened the safe, with Richardson's pistol pressed against his temple. Loomis was shaking like a tumbleweed stuck against a fence in a windstorm. He handed packets of bills to Richardson, who put them in the large canvas sack.

Hayes took the other sack, filled with money, from Reynolds, and then looked at Popper, as if waiting for instructions.

Popper looked into Loomis's office and waited.

The bookkeeper, an older woman named Georgia Henley, was the only one holding her hands up who was not shaking or trembling. Instead, Georgia was looking at the faces of the bank robbers and noting everything else that was going on.

She watched while the head clerk, Elmer Reynolds, walked up to Popper and whispered something to him. Popper's expression did not change, but when Reynolds stepped away, Zeke Popper called out to Richardson.

"Bring Loomis out here." Then, to Hayes, he said: "There's another safe, Pete, under the trapdoor behind the teller's window. Take Loomis over there and have him open it."

When Richardson led Loomis out of his office, the banker's face was blanched of all color. He looked sick, but Hayes jerked him by the arm and took him over behind the teller's cage and made him open the trapdoor and then work the combination on the safe inside. Hayes filled up another bag with money from the floor safe.

Georgia Henley studied all the faces and yet showed no sign that she was doing this. Behind her glasses, her eyes seemed vacant as marbles, but she was taking everything in.

"Where else you got money put away, Loomis?" Popper asked.

"That's not my money," Loomis said.

"Oh, I'll bet you got plenty hid away somewheres."

"I beg of you not to steal this money. It's not mine. It belongs to the farmers and ranchers around here who worked hard for it." Loomis was close to tears. His face bore a look of anguish that caused Georgia Henley to wince.

Popper just laughed.

"You bankers prey on the good honest folks. You take their money and hide it and make money offen it," Popper said. "You're all a bunch of goddamned leeches."

Loomis said nothing. He just made a whimpering sound.

That's when Popper walked up to him and drew his knife. Loomis didn't even have time to look at it before the blade flashed in the air, like some glittering silver wand, and then his throat opened up like some hideous flower, crimson and white, and he spewed blood down the front of his starched white shirt and over his tie and then he crumpled like an empty sack and struck the floor.

The customers and the other bank employees all gasped and some brought their hands down to their faces as if to shut out the horror of what they had just witnessed.

Reynolds's face was just as blanched as Georgia Henley's and he looked sick, as if he were going to throw up. Popper nodded to Hayes, and Hayes grinned idiotically.

Hayes stepped up behind Reynolds, drew his knife and punched it twice into Reynolds's back. It was so quick, not everyone in the bank saw it. But Georgia Henley did and she sucked in a quick breath and bit her lower lip as if to keep from crying out or screaming.

Reynolds turned around, halfway around, and brought up his hands in a posture of defense. Hayes, with that same sickly smile on his face, drove his knife downward into Reynolds's chest, probably straight into the heart, and Reynolds opened his arms as if he meant to embrace Hayes. Then he, too, collapsed and hit the floor, his body quivering all over as if he had been electrified.

"That's all, folks," Popper said. "You tell that toad-suckin' sheriff of your'n that he'd better not come after us lessen he wants to wind up gutted like these two no-goods."

When the three outlaws emerged from the bank, they were carrying bags full of money and Popper had Veronica with him. Her face was white, as if it had been dusted with flour, and she had a bruise on her cheek. That's when one of the witnesses noticed that the men had an extra horse. Popper forced Veronica to mount that one and the bandits rode off. They passed the tavern and all of them opened up with their rifles and shotguns. Men standing near the door were shot. Some were killed, others wounded. There was blood flowing everywhere, and the others inside, who had ducked for cover, remained in a state of confusion for several moments.

The sheriff was not hit by bullets, but he had his hands full tending to the wounded, checking the dead, and then interviewing witnesses. There were two people dead at the bank, Mr. Bertrand Loomis, the manager, and the teller, Mr. Elmer Reynolds.

It was Georgia Henley who told the sheriff that Reynolds had been employed by the bank for a year, and that he had been a guard before that at Huntsville State Prison. She suspected that Elmer had known the bank robbers at the prison and told them all about the bank and that's why they had robbed it.

"How do you know all this, Georgia?" the sheriff asked.

"Elmer is my nephew," she said. "I saw the way those robbers looked at him when they were here. They knew him all right. I don't know why they had to kill poor Elmer."

"I do, Georgia. Those boys are greedy. They didn't want to share the money."

That's when Georgia Henley broke down and, for the first time since the robbery began, lost her composure.

3

Felicia Redmond had already washed the breakfast dishes and put them away by the time her husband, Joby, and their two sons, Mark and Forrest, had finished their chores and were setting out to work the cattle on the south forty, a pasture well beyond the stand of tall pines that divided their property in half. The pines acted as a windbreak and kept the pasture smells from wafting to the house, something Felicia had insisted on when they purchased the small ranch near Gilmet, Texas, a couple of years after the war.

She looked out the window and saw Joby on his tall horse, a chestnut gelding, which stood sixteen hands high and was Joby's favorite mount. His dark silhouette stood out against the pastel backdrop of morning sky, his face obscured, but his outline etched against the morning itself, as if he were cloaked in a silence of his own making. He had stopped the horse and was turned in the saddle, beckoning to the boys. She smiled and that smile was part of her radiance even in the hazy half-light of the birthing dawn. The boys were always late for everything, but Joby had patience with them. He beckoned to the boys to hurry up, but he did not yell at them. That articulate hand of his stretched across, and broke, the silence of that moment carved out of the stillness.

She had been about to go back to their bedroom and dress for her day in the garden. She was still wearing her nightgown and a tattered and faded cotton robe that Joby disliked. But she felt comfortable in it. They were like the old slippers she wore, long overdue for retirement to the trash, but they felt good on her small feet.

"Why don't you let me buy you a new gown, Felicia," Joby was always saying. "And a pretty robe. Pink, maybe, or blue."

"Oh, Joby, we can find a better use for our money. Besides, I'm used to these night things. Don't you think I'm still pretty even in my old nightgown?"

"Sure, Felicia, you're the prettiest thing in Texas, sugar. I just thought you might feel better with some new pretties to wear."

Felicia sighed and walked out on the porch to wave good-bye to her husband and sons. She didn't always do that, but for some reason, she wanted to that morning, and besides, there was no hurry to get dressed. She had all day to work in the garden. She had packed lunches for Joby and the boys and she knew she would not see them again until nightfall.

The front door slammed behind her as she stepped outside. It had a good spring on it, one that Joby had made himself out of wire and a lead sash weight.

The boys rode out of the barn toward their father. She was proud of both of them, and both of them would probably be taller than their father. Joby wasn't a short man, but he was not tall, either. He had to stretch to come up to five feet ten inches. But he was strong, and both tough and tender in touch and thought, qualities she admired in him, or in any man, for that matter.

She waved at the boys and they waved back. Then Joby looked at her and she waved at him. He smiled, and she smiled back. That smile of his. It made something melt inside her heart and set her senses to tingling. Mark had that same smile, and Forrest, too, sometimes, when he lost his shyness. Mark favored his father in many ways, while Forrest seemed more like her, shy and reserved, quiet, thoughtful. Mark was the wild one, like his father.

"See you, Felicia," Joby called. "See you at supper."

"You be careful, Joby. Boys, you mind your pa."

"Yes'm," the boys chorused and she laughed because they both had different pitches to their voices and they sounded in harmony like those men who sang in the quartets down at the barbershop on Saturday afternoons. Forrest was almost eighteen, the eldest, while Mark was just a few months past his sixteenth birthday.

"Come on boys," Joby said. "That sun'll be up soon and you'll be stuck to your saddles before we get to the cattle yonder."

"We're comin', Pa," Mark said, a sour tone in his voice. Felicia knew he was still half asleep. It took more than strong coffee to wake Mark up. But, when the sun rose, he would be more alive than his brother.

They were like flowers, she thought. One liked the sun, the other took to the shade and bloomed mostly at night. She was glad they were different. If she had wanted them to be alike, she would have prayed to have had twins.

She was still waving long after the boys and Joby had turned around and were riding away. For some reason, she felt sad that they were leaving. The sun had just barely cleared the horizon and she wondered if she had become suddenly melancholy because of the predawn darkness.

She brought her hand back down. There was no longer anyone watching her wave good-bye.

Yet, for some reason, Felicia ran down the porch steps and to the gate of the little picket fence that surrounded the house and began waving again.

"Good-bye, Joby, good-bye Forrest and Mark. See you at supper."

But she knew they hadn't heard her. They were circling the large pond that was even now taking on a glint from the rising sun, the waters turning gold and amber and vermilion, like a liquid painting that was constantly changing colors. And she could smell the scent of the young alfalfa coming from one of the hay fields and the faint fragrance of honeysuckle and mint that grew around the well just beyond the picket fence. Joby had built trellises on three sides to give the well some shade and keep the water cool. Soon, she knew, the hummingbirds would be at the blossoms and the bees at the clover growing in still another pasture beyond the lake on the western side.

Felicia watched until her men were mere specks on the horizon, and then they were beyond the tall pines and just winked out of sight. It was then that she felt a wave of sadness engulf her, as if she had lost them forever. As if she would never see them again.

"Silly," she said aloud, and heaved a sigh. She turned from the gate and walked back up on the porch. She looked one last time at the spot on the horizon where she had last seen Joby and the boys and then drew a deep breath and opened the door.

She walked to the kitchen and checked the firebox. She added more sticks of kindling. She would need the coals when she did the ironing after she had dressed. She liked to iron in the morning when it was cool and the garden too wet from the night dew to work. She took pride in the way she organized her days and always made sure that her men never had a hint of how much she had accomplished by the time they returned home at night.

Before going into the bedroom to dress, Felicia opened the cupboard beneath the sideboard and pulled out a can she used for trash. Then she got the iron off the counter, opened it and held it over the trash can and shook out all the ashes. Later, when she did her ironing, she would put hot coals inside the iron and close it. In wintertime, she also used the iron to warm their sheets at night before they went to bed.

In the bedroom, Felicia brushed her long, dark hair, then combed it all out. She knew she would have to braid it one of these days when the summer got too hot, but for now she pulled her tresses together and clamped them high, just above her neck, with a barrette. She dressed quickly, in a skirt and blouse, and put on comfortable shoes and socks.

When she walked out on the back porch to look at the garden, she saw that the tomatoes and corn and beans were still heavy with dew.

She walked back inside and got the ironing board out of the cupboard, set it up by the kitchen table. Then she went to the hamper and brought out the clothes she had taken down from the line the night before. She set the clothes for ironing on the table, then filled a large bowl from the water pitcher on the counter. She set that on the kitchen table, then began separating the clothes, folding and stacking them in the order she would iron them.

She was reaching for the iron to fill it with the hot coals from the firebox when she heard the sound of hoofbeats coming down the road toward the house.

A strange feeling came over Felicia just then. They did not get many visitors and this wasn't the sound of just a horse or two, but of many horses.

Before she could get to the front room to look out, Felicia heard the hoofbeats come to an abrupt stop. She peered through the front window and saw five men dismount next to the well. A woman still sat atop one of the horses. The woman looked somewhat familiar.

Five men and a woman. That was strange enough, Felicia thought. But who was the woman with them? And, why did she not dismount? One of the men looked directly at Felicia and she drew back quickly. But she knew the man had seen her. They were all wearing guns and they had rifles in the scabbards attached to their saddles.

4

THE YEARLING WHITE-FACED BULL CHARGED, ITS HEAD LOWered, its short thick horns aimed for a disemboweling blow at Joby's crotch. The bull, blind as a Kentucky cave bat, could not see the man, but could smell and hear him. Joby yelled and scrambled away, toward the fence, running a zigzag course like a scared rabbit.

Some of the cattle on Joby Redmond's small ranch had the pinkeye. He and his boys were separating those that were infected from the main herd, driving them into a small corral that he had built when he first bought the land.

Now the work was dangerous, as Mark and Forrest entered the corral with latigos and roped each infected cow. Since most of the cattle were blind, they were spooky and would charge at any sound and try to hook one of the boys with deadly horns.

"Scaredy cat," Mark chided his father.

"Rope him, Forrest," Joby replied as he reached the fence rails. "Hurry."

"Pa, that ain't nothin' but a bull calf," Forrest said, with a grin. "He won't hurt you none."

But Forrest had snaked out his rope and built a loop, and he flung the noose over the bull's head and dug in his boot heels and took up the slack, jerking the young bull sideways just as the horns came within an inch or two of raking his father's buttocks. The bull shook its head and spun around. Then it charged Forrest, who wisely threw the bitter end of the rope at the bull and scrambled to the fence and climbed the rails just in time to avoid getting butted.

Mark made a loop in his latigo and snaked it over the bull's head, then snubbed the end of the rope to a post. As the bull charged him, he ran around it and grabbed up Forrest's rope and ran to another post in the opposite direction, ran it around a post and pulled hard. When the slack went out, he had the bull secured with two taut ropes. He looked up at his father and grinned wide.

"You can climb down now, Pa. This little ol' bull ain't gonna hurt you none, I reckon."

"Mark, you got a sassy mouth," Joby said.

"You want me to put the medicine in the bull's eyes, Pa?" Forrest asked, a mischievous lilt to his question. "I ain't afraid of him none."

"You can just shut your flap, too, Forrest," Joby said, climbing down from the fence. "I sure don't know where you boys got your sassiness. Probably from your mother."

"We got it from you, Pa," Mark said. "You're always sassing Ma back."

"Yeah, in a whisper," Forrest said. "So's she won't hear him."

Both boys laughed and Joby pretended to put on a scowl as he reached in his pocket for the tin of salve he was using to doctor the pinkeye. He ran down one rope, keeping it taut, and put an arm around the bull's boss and bent its head back. The bull struggled against him, trying to toss its head, but Joby held the horns in a firm grip. He dug a finger into the salve and stuck some in one of the bull's eyes, then jumped back, releasing the bull.

The bull twisted and pawed the ground, tossing its head from side to side, trying to break free of the two ropes. It snorted and began to buck and kick as Joby walked around behind it.

"Lively one, ain't he?" Joby said. "He'll make a fine seed bull in a couple of years."

"Want us to turn him loose, Pa, so you can play with him?" Mark asked.

"I'll turn you loose in a minute," Joby said, working his way back up behind the bull's horns. Again, he took the flat tin from his pocket and dug a finger into it, then rubbed the salve into the calf's other eye. His hands were quick, but the young bull reacted immediately. It threw its head up and back down, trying to hook Joby. Its horns swept in a semicircle, but Joby jumped back, out of the way.

"Pa," Mark asked, "what is that stuff you put in their eyes, anyway?"

"It's a mixture of tree mold, mud and wagon wheel grease. Feller in Gilmet makes it up. I think he mashes up tree moss and some other stuff to put in it. He won't tell me all that he puts in it. I bought that big bucket of it over there and put what I need in this snuff tin. I've still got enough in the tin to coat another couple of head."

"The cattle don't like it none," Forrest said. "And it sure don't help their blindness."

"It keeps the sun out of their eyes, keeps the bugs from getting in them," Joby said. "Feller in town, Willie Baber, swears by it. He's doctored a lot of cattle with pinkeye and swears by it."

"What do you want to do with this calf?" Mark asked.

"Turn him out, then rope me another one," his father said.

The two boys worked well together. Forrest opened the gate and kept the other cattle from running out, while Mark shook loose the ropes and let the doctored calf run out to pasture.

They were starting on the second calf of the day when they all heard a scream from far away. It was such a brief scream that it took several seconds for the sound to register.

"What in hell was that?" Mark asked.

"Sounded like a scream," Forrest said.

Joby put a hand to his ear and listened intently, but none of them heard it again. "It sounded like it was coming from the house," Joby said.

"I thought it came from the woods," Forrest said.

"I couldn't tell where it was coming from," Mark said.

"Mark, you'd better saddle up and ride to the house. See if everything is all right."

"Aw, Pa, do I have to?"

"Do it," Joby said. "Don't argue with me."

"Why do I always have to do the hard stuff?" Mark asked.

"We can do without you for a while, Mark," Joby said. "It could be nothing, but I want it checked out."

"Do you think it was Ma?" Forrest asked.

"If I thought it was her, I'd be riding hell for leather myself," Joby said.

Mark slouched away, crawling through the rails of the corral. He walked over to his hobbled horse that was grazing in a copse of shade trees some distance away. He threw his saddle on and rode off toward the house. He looked back and Joby urged him with a hand gesture to hurry. Mark put his horse into a gallop and was soon lost from view.

"What do you think that was, Pa?" Forrest asked, as he snaked out his rope to make a loop so he could catch the next calf that needed doctoring.

Joby frowned. He tried to remember what the scream had sounded like, but the memory was already fading from his mind. The scream had not sounded like any particular person. He thought it might have been a woman's scream, but now he could not be sure. He had never heard Felicia scream, so he had nothing to compare the sound to, now that he thought of it. What would cause Felicia to scream? And, was it a woman's scream? He didn't know the answer to that, either. Could it have been a hawk? Or an eagle? Or some animal? Joby did not know, and now he could barely remember what it had sounded like.

Joby watched as Forrest stalked the next calf, another yearling, with shorter horns than the last one. He wondered if Forrest could handle the task by himself or if he should put another rope around the calf's neck.

"Do you want me to put another rope on that calf, Forrest?"

"Naw, I don't think this one will give us any trouble."

Forrest circled the calf, widening the loop in his rope as he walked, making little noise with his feet. Just as he braced himself to hurl the rope, a gunshot broke the silence. Forrest froze and the rope went limp, the loop collapsing to the ground. The calf spooked at the sound and whirled around to face the danger it felt. It dropped its head, preparing to charge at the place where the loop had fallen.

Joby muttered a curse under his breath.

"Was that Mark?" Forrest asked.

"He doesn't have a gun with him. Neither do we," Joby said.

"It sounded like it came form the house."

"It damned sure did," Joby agreed.

Then they both heard a series of shots, all coming from the house, beyond the pasture, beyond the trees. Joby scrambled through the rails and headed for their horses.

"Come on, Forrest," Joby yelled. "Something's going on."

Forrest slid between two rails and was hot on his father's heels as more gunshots sounded in the distance.

Joby knew exactly where the sounds of gunshots were coming from and his stomach roiled with a sickness that sent bile rising in his throat. He carried no weapon, and neither did either of his sons. Since the war, he had not used either his pistol, rifle or scattergun except for hunting and while he had taught his wife, Felicia, and his sons, Mark and Forrest, how to shoot, he knew that those shots he'd heard were not from any of the guns he owned.

With a deepening sense of dread, Joby rode past Forrest at a furious gallop, the sickness in him growing like some paralyzing force, constricting his throat so that he could not even yell or scream. He only knew that he had to get to the house no matter what he might see there. He rode under a blue sky that somehow had turned pitch black and the sickness inside him was suddenly turning to fear.

5

JOBY RODE PAST THE TALL PINES AND INTO THE OPEN, FOLlowed by Forrest, who had almost caught up with him. As he was rounding the last stand of trees, he heard distant hoofbeats, and he saw a cloud of dust above the road that passed in front of his house.

Joby rode into an eerie silence as the hoofbeats faded away, and his heart seemed to sink as he saw Mark ahead of him, lying on the ground behind his fallen horse, as if they had both been shot dead.

As Joby approached the downed horse and his son, Mark, his throat constricted as his stomach roiled with a clawing fear. Yet he knew he could not allow that fear to paralyze him. If Mark was alive and needed help, he must be ready to render aid. He knew he must rise above his personal feelings and be strong enough to overcome the fear.

"Mark," he called, as he rode close.

"Pa, what happened?" Forrest asked. "Is Mark . . ."

Forrest could not bring himself to put the thought into words. Joby knew how his son felt. No person was ever prepared for sudden, unexpected tragedy.

"I don't know, Forrest," Joby said. "Let's not think the worst."

"Oh, Pa, I think he's dead," Forrest said.

Joby scanned Mark's body, looking for blood, for signs of life. Then he looked at the horse, Whitey, the horse Mark used when they worked out in the fields. Whitey lay on its side, a large pool of blood beneath its carcass. Joby's stomach knotted up and he blinked back tears that had sprung up in his eyes unbidden.

"Mark," Joby breathed, his voice barely audible, the word like a prayer on his lips.

Joby swung down out of the saddle and rushed to his son's side. He knelt beside Mark and bent his head down, placing his ear next to his son's mouth. He listened, and he heard breathing. Joby raised up and took his son's head in his hands. "Mark, Mark," he said. "Can you hear me?"

Forrest rode up, then, and leaped from the saddle to join his father beside Mark. "Is he—is he dead?" Forrest asked, a tremor in his voice.

"No, he's alive."

"Thank God."

"Mark, wake up," Joby pleaded. He tapped his son on the cheek to revive him. Mark's eyelids fluttered. A sound escaped his throat and he swallowed. Then his eyes remained open, but they were glazed and virtually sightless.

"Mark, are you hurt?" his father asked. "Can you hear me?"

"I—I—uh, what happened?" Mark stuttered. "My horse . . ."

"Never mind the horse. Are you hurt?"

Mark blinked a couple of times and then the glaze fled from his eyes and he focused on his father's face.

"Pa. They shot my horse. I fell off when Whitey went down."

"I know. You got knocked out. Can you sit up?"

"Yeah, I think so." Mark sat up. He looked groggy, but Joby knew he was going to be all right. "Pa, they shot my horse out from under me."

"I know. Whitey is dead."

"I think they killed all of our horses," Mark said. "They were out by the stables, a bunch of 'em, and I heard the horses raisin' a ruckus. Then one of the men pointed a rifle at me and shot my horse."

"Whoever did it rode away," Forrest said. "Did you see 'em, Pa?"

"I saw them."

"Who were they?" Mark asked.

Joby shook his head. "I don't know. But your mother is all alone at the house. I've got to go check on her right away."

"She's not alone," Mark said.

"Huh?"

"I saw Auntie Dolores's horse when I was riding up."

"My sister's here?" Joby asked.

"Well, I saw her horse. But, I think they shot Rose, too." Rose was his sister's bay mare. Joby looked off toward the house. There was a dead horse out front and it looked like his sister's.

"Climb on my horse, Mark. We'll pack double going in."

"Yes, sir," Mark said.

Joby helped his son to his feet and helped him lift his boot into the stirrup. He shoved his son up and Mark swung onto the back of his father's horse. Joby mounted his horse and Mark put his arms around his father's waist as he had done since he was a small boy.

Joby's dread thickened and deepened as he rode toward the house. There was a silence about it that he didn't like, an emptiness that he could feel in his heart and in his gut. Where was Felicia? Where was his sister? And who were those men who had shot and killed all his horses and Dolores's horse?

As Joby and his sons drew closer to the house, the silence became almost palpable. The house took on an aspect of horror, sitting out there on the plain that he had cleared with his bare hands so many years ago. Something terrible had happened here, Joby knew, long before those men started killing his horses.

"Pa, where's Ma?" Mark asked. "She always comes out when we come home."

"I don't know, Mark. Just brace yourself."

"Brace myself? For what?"

"For anything," Joby said.

Joby reined in his horse and slid out of the saddle. Mark hopped down right afterward. Forrest rode up, a look of bewilderment on his face, his mouth open as if he had been struck dumb.

"Where's Ma?" Forrest asked, suddenly regaining his voice as he stepped down from the saddle.

The scream tore at their hearts and senses like some unearthly beast with sharp claws. The scream was piercing, high-pitched as if it came from some register not on the human scale, but from somewhere beyond comprehension. There was something primitive in it, something primordial, as if it emanated from some distant jungle that was ancient and African, or Asian. It was a scream beyond any horror any of them had ever known, even Joby, who had been in the war and heard screams that still haunted his deepest and most complex dreams.

The three of them turned toward the house, and there, in the doorway, stood a woman, stark naked, her hands raised and pressed against the doorjamb for support. Her legs were streaming with streaks of blood and her face glistened with tears that had left grimy tracks down her cheeks. Her body was covered with vivid purple bruises.

"Boys, turn your heads," Joby said softly. "Now."

It was Dolores, Joby's sister, and she only stopped

screaming long enough to take in a breath. And then she screamed again and the boys looked up, despite their father's command, and their gazes fixed on their aunt as the hackles rose on the backs of their necks and their stomachs quivered with fear.

"Damn it," Joby snapped, "don't look at her."

And then he was running toward the doorway, running through the scream that whipped at him like a ferocious lash unleashed by some demon from hell.

6

JOBY RUSHED TO THE DOORWAY AND SWOOPED HIS SISTER UP into his arms and carried her back inside the house. She screamed even louder when he grabbed her and her anguish ripped through his heart like a knife.

"Dolores," he crooned, "it's all right. I'll take care of you. Calm down."

He sat her on the divan in the front room and took off his shirt, slipped her arms through the sleeves and buttoned it up as she sat there, rocking, staring off into space, staring at nothing that was there.

Joby knelt down in front of her and looked at the blood streaking her legs. He winced, not yet able to form the thought that was lurking at the back brink of his mind. He thought of Felicia and wondered if she, too, had been violated and was lying somewhere in the house, unconscious or dead.

"Joby," Dolores murmured. "Oh, Joby, they took Felicia."

"They took Felicia?"

Dolores nodded. She looked so small and helpless, so frail in his faded blue chambray shirt. But she was only a girl, just barely sixteen, Mark's age. She lived with his mother, Rosalind, near Gilmet. His father had died a good five years ago, of consumption. But his father had left enough money for Rosalind and Dolores to get by. She was still in school and he generally saw her and his mother on Sundays when they all went to church together.

"What happened?" he asked, trying to quell the quaver in his voice. "Who hurt you? What about Ma?"

"Poor Ma. They beat her pretty bad. And then they grabbed me. At first I thought they were with Ronnie. She was with them. Then I saw that she was a prisoner. They slapped me and brought me here and then that one, he—he raped me."

"Raped you?"

"He said he was going to do the same thing to your wife and he wanted you to know."

Dolores put her head down and covered her face with her hands. Then she began sobbing. Her body shook with the force of her emotions, as if she were possessed by demons. Joby knew that his sister was on the verge of hysteria and he put an arm over her heaving shoulders to calm her down.

"What was the name of this man?" he asked, his voice barely above a whisper.

But Dolores could not answer. Instead, her sobbing increased and she crumpled as her head fell lower toward her lap. She drew her knees up as if she were trying to curl up into a ball, like some animal trying to conceal itself from attack. She looked pathetic, Joby thought, as if something had broken inside her and taken away her girlhood, her dignity and her pride in herself.

"There, there," he said. "It's all right. Those men have gone and I'm here, Sis. I'll take care of you."

"Oh, Joby," she wailed and began to cry even harder.

"Cry it all out, but I need to know who those men were and why they picked on you."

"Uh huh," she sobbed, and Joby could see that she was trying to pull herself together.

"I've got to go after those men, Sis. I've got to get Felicia away from them."

"I—I know."

"They're getting farther and farther away."

She did not reply. Instead, he could see that she was trying to stop crying. She looked up at him with pleading eyes, eyes that were red-rimmed and filled with tears. She nodded and he patted her shoulder with one hand, nodded back to her with sympathy.

"They—the others—they called him ZP."

Joby's jaw hardened and his face took on a dark cast as if she had struck some deep chord inside him that triggered an indecipherable anger.

A curse escaped his lips and Dolores's mouth opened in surprise.

"You know him?" she asked.

Joby shook his head, but it had nothing to do with a negative answer. He looked at Dolores and sighed deeply as if he were carrying a great burden that he had never shared with anyone.

"I thought he was in prison," Joby said. "I thought he'd be in prison for the rest of his life."

"A convict? And, you—you know him?" Dolores was starting to come out of her crying spell.

"It's a long story, sugar. I knew him in the war. We fought in the same outfit, for a time. But . . ."

"But what?" She sniffled and wiped her nose with one of his shirtsleeves that was dangling, armless, from her shoulders.

"Do you remember that dog we had, Dolores? The one our pa called Chico? A tan mongrel we took in."

"I remember him. He became our pet. What's that got to do with that—that man who raped me?"

"Yes, Chico became a pet. But he had been mistreated, and maybe he had been out in the wild too long before he came to us. Whatever it was, he started to go bad. At first, he got after the little chicks. We came home from the fields one day to find almost all of our pullets dead, their necks all wrung and scattered about like trash all over the yard."

"Was that Chico?"

"Yes," Joby said, nodding.

"How did you know it was him?"

"We didn't want to believe it, at first. When we got after him, he cowered and slunk around and we all felt sorry for him. You said that a coyote must have gotten into the henhouse. That it couldn't have been Chico."

"I remember that. Not too well, though."

"No, but it got worse after that. When the pullets were all dead and gone, Chico started going after the grown hens and the roosters and he killed every one of 'em. Then he started snarling at Ma and one day he went after her with his fangs all bared and he was going to bite her. That's when Pa got the scattergun and shot Chico dead."

"I cried about that. I hated Pa for that. I still don't understand what you're trying to say, Joby."

"I'm trying to say that ZP was like that dog, Chico. He went bad. He turned plumb mean and he deserted the army, and he met up with some other deserters and they started robbing people and raping women and he got caught and sent down to Huntsville Prison."

"And you knew this man, Joby?"

"I'm the man who tracked him down. I'm the one who sent him and his friends to prison."

Dolores gasped. She looked at her brother oddly, almost in disbelief.

"I never knew that. Did Ma and Pa know?"

"I never told them. I never told anyone. It was at the end of the war and I was commissioned to track down ZP and his men and bring them in for court-martial."

"And you did all that?"

Joby nodded. He drew in a deep breath. He held it and then let it out in a rush.

"Then why is this man on the loose?"

Joby shook his head. "I don't know. He must have escaped. From prison."

"He's an animal."

"I know."

Joby thought back to the suffering his parents and other families had undergone, during and after the war. Men like Popper took advantage of folks who had lost their wealth and their livelihoods with their sacrifices. His own parents had been rich, and the war had reduced them to paupers. But men like ZP and his cronies forced them to undergo further indignities. Company K of the Second Texas Infantry had fought many battles and lost a lot of men, men better than ZP and those who deserted with him. Joby thought of the men he had known and who had died. He had thought of them often through the long, hard years after the war, and he had thought of the battles, too, and the slaughter, the senseless slaughter of hundreds and thousands of men who did not come back from the war, who died at Shiloh, at the two battles they fought in Corinth, at Talahatchie, Greenwood, Chickasaw, Bayou and Vicksburg.

"What's the matter, Joby?" Dolores asked when he didn't say anything for several seconds.

"I've got to go after them, Dolores. I've got to get Felicia back and . . ."

"And what?"

Joby's jaw stiffened and a dark hard look came into his eyes.

"And nothing."

There was a silence between brother and sister.

"You're going to kill them, aren't you?" she said.

Joby drew in a long breath and let it out through his nostrils.

"Every goddamned one of 'em, sugar."

Dolores shivered involuntarily. She knew her brother had been in the war. She had watched him leave when she was just a tadpole of a girl and she had seen him come back as a stranger, a man who had left home a boy and, through the mysterious alchemy of war and horror and suffering, he had returned a man, a man with sharp piercing eyes that looked right through you, and beyond, a man who never spoke much, never said anything about the war, but just looked as if he had been to hell and back, all burned inside, all burned in mind and body and scarred on his skin and on his very soul.

She touched her brother's arm and patted it in sympathy.

"You'll get Felicia back," she said. "And you'll make those men pay for what they did to us. For what they did to me and Ma."

"And for a whole hell of a lot more," Joby whispered, so softly that Dolores had to strain to hear him.

"I—I'm going to bathe," she said. "I've got to wash that horrible man off of me. Look at the blood. Look at what he did to me."

She hung her head in shame and Joby held her very tightly and squeezed his eyes shut so that he might stop the tears that threatened to come.

But he could not, and Joby began to cry and they held each other tightly for several moments as they both wept together in the silence of the room.

7

Mark and Forrest walked around the barn and corral in a daze. Dead horses lay strewn from the front of the barn to the workout corral, their bodies swelling in the sun and swarming with the shiny bodies of bluebottle flies. Joby came around the corner of the house and saw the slaughter. Mark turned toward him, his face a study in horror and bewilderment. Then he doubled over and began vomiting.

"Where's our ma?" Forrest asked, in a daze, his voice sounding disembodied, hollow, as if he, too, were bewildered to the point of senselessness.

Joby stood next to Mark and put a comforting hand on his shoulder.

"Boys, this is all bad news. Your ma has been kidnapped by some bad men and your aunt Do is all torn up inside."

"What happened to Aunt Do?" Forrest asked.

"I'll tell you later, Forrest. Now is not the time. Mark, you want some water?"

Mark shook his head and then convulsed into dry heaves. His body shook under the contractions and his voice made a hoarse croaking sound. Then he straightened up and shook his head as if to clear it. He walked away from the vomit to get far from the smell of his stomach contents. Joby held his breath and walked away, too.

The scene there looked like a battlefield, but a battlefield like none other he had ever seen. There were no human corpses. It was, though, as if an army had passed through and all that was left were the dead horses. As if the defeated army had taken their dead away and vanished. Joby felt the hackles rise on the back of his neck.

The eeriness of it took him back to Shiloh and Vicksburg, and he could almost see the white smoke of battle lingering in the grasses when the cannons and the rifles had gone silent. The armies carried their dead soldiers away during the night, but the horses lay steaming in the sun, their bodies bloating in the heat, their vacant eyes alive with flies, their hides twitching from the assault of scissoring insects, their carcasses adding to the stench of human death as they gave up their scents like the morning vapors of dew rising from the grasses and the morning glories.

"See which horses they killed, Forrest. Give me a count."

"We know they got Whitey, and Rose, Aunt Do's horse and . . ."

"Make the count," Joby repeated.

"They didn't get Blackie, Jules or Champ," Mark said. "They're over yonder in them trees." He pointed. Joby couldn't see them, but there was good pasture there and some of the horses liked to stay in the shade where he had left a stand of pines and oaks and sweet gum trees.

"I don't see all the horses here," Joby said. "See if you can round up the couple we may have left. We'll need them."

"We goin' somewhere?" Forrest asked.

"We are," Joby said.

"Where?" asked Mark.

"To get your mother back."

"When?"

"As soon as we finish here and break out the guns and ammunition we're going to need to take with us. And we'll have to pack grub and bedrolls. It might be a long ride."

"What are we going to do with these dead horses?" Mark asked.

"Find Jethro if you can. We'll use him to haul these carcasses out away from the house and burn 'em," Joby said.

Mark's face turned ashen at the thought, but he started walking off toward the grove of trees, calling, "Mule, hey mule. Jethro, boy."

Forrest began to count the dead horses. When he emerged from the barn, Joby could see that he had gotten sick inside and thrown up his breakfast.

"Now, you put up our horses on the other side of the house. I don't want them to see these dead ones," Joby said.

"What are you going to do?" Forrest asked.

"I'm going to see how Do is doing and then start getting some guns together."

"I'll help you when I finish tying up the horses."

"Good. I hope we have enough ammunition to take with us."

"We should. You always buy extra when we go into Gilmet."

It was so, Joby knew. Every chance he got, he bought ammunition for the rifles and pistols. Civilization was a fine thing, but the war had taught him that nothing was certain and that a lot of men had violent streaks. Men like Popper and Corporal Roy Botts, and Private Richard Lee Richardson and Private Pete Hayes, men he had tracked down before and who had been sent to the state prison in Huntsville.

"Yeah, I reckon we'll have enough."

"Do Mark and I get to shoot, too?"

"I hope it doesn't come to that."

"But, if there's a fight . . ."

Joby held his breath. He had not told his sons about the war. He had taught them to shoot, to hunt and to fish. But he had never spoken to them about shooting a man, never told them how it was to kill a man. Or where to shoot a man to kill him quick, or just wound him, if that was called for, which was damned seldom.

The truth was, he told himself, told himself right then and there, he hated war and he hoped his sons would never have to go through what he had gone through. He hoped that neither Mark nor Forrest would ever have to shoot a man, much less kill one. His stomach roiled at the thought of either of his boys ever having to draw blood, and worse, ever having to take away a man's life. For, Joby reasoned, taking a man's life, depriving him of breath and family and, yes, love, was a terrible thing to do, a terrible thing to live with for the rest of a man's life.

Joby started walking back to the house.

"When are we goin' after those men, Pa?" Forrest called to him.

"As soon as I take Auntie Do back home and get back here. Maybe tonight."

"Boy, I can't wait."

"You can wait," Joby whispered, but it was not loud enough so that Forrest could hear him. The boy was too eager to ride into something he didn't understand. ZP was a killer and, worse, he had no conscience. Joby was sure he had gone to his house deliberately to get his little sister and come by here to kidnap Felicia. He meant to pay Joby back for sending him to prison, something ZP had vowed to do when he was sentenced.

Maybe he should have killed all of them before they ever had a court trial. Just shot them down like the dogs they were. But he hadn't been raised that way and the army sure as hell wouldn't have condoned such an act of vengeance. At least General Van Dorn would not have tolerated such an assassination. He believed in justice, but he also believed in honor. And so did I, Joby thought. Then. But this was personal. His sister and his wife had both been violated. At least Do had, and he had no doubt that ZP would take his savage hatred for Joby out on Felicia.

And laugh while he did it, Joby thought.

He had seen and heard that laugh before.

In that moment, Joby made a decision. He could not take his sons with him when he went after Popper and the others. They were too young, and they had no experience. He would be putting them in danger. Neither was a match for Popper or any of his men.

No, he decided. He would have to do this alone. He would have to solve his own problems and leave his sons out of it. And if something happened to him, well, he had lived a full life. But the boys were just barely starting theirs.

No, he would not take them on this quest for justice. He would hunt down the men who had kidnapped his wife and make them pay for what they had done to her and to his sister.

And, he would do it all by himself.

"I'm coming, Felicia," he said to himself, and it sounded in his ears like a prayer. But it was a vow.

A vow he meant to keep.

8

Dolores was drying her hair when Joby entered the house. She had already bathed in the big tub on the back porch and put her dress back on. It was one he had bought for her in Gilmet a few months ago and still looked nice on her.

"I'm going to take you back to Ma's, Do," he said.

"I'm worried about her, Joby. Those bad men mauled her pretty badly, and when we were leaving, one of the men went back inside. He came back outside and nodded to that Popper man. And Popper smiled. So I don't know what he did in there. I didn't see Ma after they took me out of the house. She must be frantic by now."

Joby felt something hard and cold sink into his stomach, like a leaden sash weight that had been in the snow. Dolores didn't know these men like he did. She didn't know what they were capable of doing. She didn't know how heartless they were. Nor did she know that these were men who had no conscience.

"Are you ready to go, Sis?"

"Yes. I'm not shaking anymore. Not outside, anyway."

"I'm sorry this happened to you, Do."

There was more he wanted to say, but he could see that even his simple expression of sorrow over what had happened to his sister was having an effect on her. Her lips began quivering and he could see that she was trying to fight back the emotions she was feeling.

"I—it's hard to get out of my mind," she said. "That man. That awful, awful man."

He walked over and put his arms around Dolores and squeezed her tightly. She shuddered once and then patted him on the back.

"I—I'm all right," she said. "Let's go. I'm worried about our mother."

He thought, *So am I.* But he did not say it aloud. Dolores walked out of the room to take the towel to the back porch and hang it up on a line to dry. She returned in a few minutes, patting her auburn hair. She had Joby's hazel eyes, inherited from their father, but she had her mother's soft silky hair.

"I'll get over this," she said softly, as if to herself.

"I know you will. You've got the Redmond blood in your veins."

She looked at him, then, her eyes filled with a sudden sadness. He raised his eyebrows in a questioning look of his own.

"Joby, do you remember what Ma always said when we made a mistake, or if something went wrong and we howled or complained? Like when I broke a dish her own grandma had given her. I was crying and wailing and feeling real dumb and like a criminal."

"It was just a cup," Joby said. "An old cup."

"But our ma set store by it and I felt real bad. I thought she was going to give me a whipping. But she said, 'Do, darlin', don't cry over spilt milk.' "

"Yes, that's what ma always says. She didn't believe in

trying to fix something that couldn't be fixed, or trying to change the past."

"But, Joby, do you remember what you always said to me when I broke something or did something I couldn't mend?"

"Yes, I know what I said, Do. Same thing, really."

"Well, maybe, but I liked it better. You said, 'You can't put a raindrop back in the sky.' "

"No, you can't."

"Well, that's the way I feel about what happened to me. I can't change that. I can't put that raindrop, the one that fell on me, back in the sky."

"No, you can't."

As Joby and Dolores were about to leave, Mark came in through the back door and clumped out into the front room.

"Hi, Aunt Do," Mark said, a sheepish look on his face. "Pa, I found the horses and the mule."

"Were they where we expected them to be?"

"No, I reckon the shooting scared 'em. They was all scattered in those pineys over back of the pond."

"All right. Tell me which horses are still alive."

"Lupe's still alive," Mark said. "Thank God. She's my favorite riding horse."

"I'm glad, Mark," Joby said. "How many more horses did you find alive?"

"There's the mare, Bridey, and the two four-year-olds, Cap and Monty, the ones we helped geld. And the other gelding, Jake."

"I haven't got a count from Forrest yet, but that may be it. We have seven horses left."

"Forrest's comin'. I brought the mule and the other horses up and put 'em in the corral."

"Good," Joby said. "Look after things here, will you, Mark? Your aunt Do and I are going to ride over to your grandma's and I'll be back in less than an hour."

It was only three miles to his mother's place. If everything was all right, he would not linger, but turn right around and ride back, leading the horse Dolores would ride.

"Auntie Do will ride your horse, Mark."

"Well, Lupe's a real gentle mare. She'll ride you, Aunt Do."

Dolores smiled. "I know. I used to crawl between her legs, remember? When you were first learning to ride."

Mark grinned. "That's right," he said.

"Joby, let's go," she said. She gave Mark a tentative hug and led the way out the front door. Joby followed. They went beyond the house to where the saddled horses were tied. Joby looked them over. They were not sweating yet, but the sun was high and beating down on them. His clothes would be soaked through by the time he got back from taking Dolores home. He just hoped their mother was all right. But, he didn't like the sense of dread that was beginning to build up in him like some ravenous beast sniffing at his senses, turning noon into a darkness that filled his very soul.

He was hungry, too, by then, as the sun climbed to its zenith in the sky. His and the boys' lunches were still out in the pasture, nestled under a big live oak where they had planned to stop work and eat lunch. Now his stomach was growling. He looked over at Dolores, riding next to him, to see if he could tell if she was hungry, too.

She rode well even though she was in pain. She sat easily in the saddle as if she were born to it. With her trim figure, and even with the dress on, she looked to be part of the horse, part of its rhythm and grace, not just a person sitting on a saddle and being bounced up and down with every gaited step.

Dolores saw her brother looking at her and she tried a weak smile, but it faded on her lips like something made of smoke.

"I'll end up an old maid," she said.

"What?"

"I'm no good anymore, Joby."

"What are you talking about, Do? You're still a kid."

"I'm not a virgin anymore. No man will have me."

"That's horseshit, Do. Pure horseshit."

"No, it isn't. That evil man took my maidenhead."

For a minute, Joby thought she was going to cry, but, although she puckered up her lips, no tears came. Instead, she looked almost defiant. And, maybe, he thought, that was a good sign.

"You'll be all right. Just don't think about what happened to you. I mean, don't think about it all the time."

"I can still feel the pain. I can still smell his rank odor. I can still feel his grimy hands on me."

"Stop it, Do."

"I can't help it, Joby. I can feel him inside me, too."

Joby winced with the image the thought brought to him. He couldn't think of his own sister that way. But that's just what he was doing.

"Stop talkin' that way, Do. You're only makin' things worse for yourself."

She sighed and when he looked at her he could see that her jaw was set and hard, but he could not tell if she was angry or still hurting from the memory of being raped by ZP.

"You're right, Joby," she said. "This isn't helping any, but I know what men think of women who are no longer virgins."

"Some men, maybe."

"At school, that's all the boys talk about. And the girls, too."

"The world you're going into as a woman isn't school, Dolores."

"I'm going on as an old maid. I'll wind up a spinster."

"That's just dust," he said.

"What?"

"What happened to you has just put dust in your eyes, Do. You've got to wash it out. Don't rub it in."

"There you go with your old philosopher's stuff again. Well, I can't put a raindrop back in the sky, smartypants, and I can't put my maidenhead back together like it was."

"What I said still goes. Not philosophy, darlin', but a good piece of advice."

"The dust?"

"Yeah, the dust. You can wash it out. If you rub your eyes, it will just go deeper and hurt like hell for a long time."

"Or," she said, "make me blind. To everything that happened to me. Blind."

Joby said nothing, and they rode on, heading toward the little road to their mother's house that wound through the tall pines, past a little wooded pond and an old wooden shack that had once been a way station for travelers, long before the Civil War.

And it was quiet, Joby thought, the silence like other silences he had known before, the ones just before a big battle, when the fear was knotted up inside him like a rope made of cold iron, or the silences after a battle, when the dead lay strewn among the grasses and flowers like bundles of old rags, their vacant eyes staring upward at the blue sky as if they had known that was their final destination.

9

Sheriff Tom Keller knew he had a problem. The town seemed to be in chaos. Beyond the confusion, there was anger and sorrow, and, more disconcerting and ominous, hate. Hate for the killers, the kidnappers, the robbers.

As one wag had put it, "there was no balm in Gilmet." And now, Keller was faced with a decision as he confronted what had become a raging mob, a mob bent on revenge. Men had armed themselves with everything from sickles and scythes to old caplock pistols and rusty scatterguns, pitchforks and Civil War swords. Keller faced them on the porch in front of his homely office, his real office, not the saloon, and held up his hands for silence so that he could speak.

"Sheriff, are you a-goin' to get together a posse or not?" one man shouted, as the crowd quieted down.

"Yes, you've got to hang those murderin' bastards," grumbled another man with a high-pitched, squeaky voice.

"Now, now," Keller said, "just settle down. That's what we're here for. To choose members of a posse, who will be duly sworn, according to Texas law."

A chorus of men raised their hands and shouted, "I'll go, I'll go."

Sheriff Keller made flattening motions with his hands and arms to indicate that they should all be quiet until he finished talking.

Most of the women were over at the bank or at the undertaker's. Those at the bank were washing up the blood and consoling the women clerks who were still badly shaken by the events of that morning. The women at Neal Whiting's Undertaking Parlor were washing and dressing those who had been killed. It was a sad day in Gilmet.

"What I'm going to do," Keller said, "is start weeding y'all out so's I can take only those able-bodied with me to go after those murderin' scoundrels."

The crowd started to protest, but Keller shouted them down with forceful gestures.

"Just hold on and I'll explain what we're goin' to do here. The more ruckus you raise the longer it's goin' to take and the farther away them bastards are goin' to get.

"Now, we don't have much time and some ladies are getting together enough grub to keep us goin' for a couple of days. They're over to Srimple's grocery packing our grub."

The sheriff paused and looked over the crowd of men, some wearing overalls, some looking as if they'd just woken up from a flophouse bed, others in clean pressed shirts and pants. He knew what he wanted but he had little to pick from on such short notice.

"I'm a-goin', Sheriff," one man said.

Keller fixed him with a hard gaze. It was Johnny Roland, who played the piano in the saloon. Well, he was one of those who knew how to take care of himself. He had surely handled a lot of mean drunks in his time. But he was right on the edge of the age group Keller was thinking of taking with him. He didn't want boys and he didn't want old men. Not on this ride.

"Okay, okay," Keller said. "Just let me handle this my way. And all of you shut up. You, too, Johnny."

Roland scowled, but he said nothing.

"Now, I'm goin' to do some culling," Keller said. He was a stocky, florid-faced man with pudgy jowls, long sideburns connecting to sandy-red hair and pointing to a burly, thick neck that grew out of a barrel-chested torso that was more fat than lean. With the big .45 Colt revolver on his hip, he loomed even larger than his five feet eight inches of height, and the star pinned to his vest gave him even more stature to the men standing below him in the street.

"All you boys under sixteen, go on home. Now."

Some of the boys under that age kicked at the dirt in protest and grumbled among themselves, but they turned out and walked away, thinning the pack of people by a few.

"Next," Keller went on, "those of you over forty can go on home. Take your leave, gentlemen. That means you, Charlie, and you, Claude, and four or five others I see here."

Those men left the group, and Keller sighed deeply and smacked his lips in satisfaction.

"Millpas, you're a tracker," Keller said. "I want you to come along."

Bob Millpas nodded. He was a taciturn man. But, as Keller had noted, he was a patient tracker, a hunter, and he knew the country, not only in East Texas but clear to its four borders.

"Any of you with ailments, leave now. I mean you, Joe, with your game leg, and Percy there, you've been ailin'. We can't use you now. Just go on home."

Those men left, and there were, perhaps, sixteen to eighteen men remaining. Far too many for Keller to manage.

"Uberstrasse, you want to come with us?"

"Sure, Tom. You know I do."

"I want you to bring that fast horse of yours, what's his name?"

"Eagle."

A couple of the men chuckled.

"You can laugh," Keller said, "but Tommy's Eagle can go the distance. We have to move damned fast if we're goin' to catch these jaspers, and all of you who come with me have got to bring your best mounts."

The men all nodded in unison.

"Okay, we've got Tommy Uberstrasse, Bob Millpas and Johnny Roland, for sure. Now, I need five or six more. I prefer single men, but you who really want to go and have fast, strong horses, step forward."

"I aim to go with you, Tom," said one man who was shorter than the others and whom Keller hadn't seen until he spoke up.

"That you, Dillars?"

"You know it is, Tom. I want to be in the posse."

Keller scowled. It was Roderick Dillars, all right. Dillars pushed to the front of the crowd. He was carrying a scattergun and had a small-caliber pistol in a holster attached to his belt.

"No, Rod, you ain't comin' with us."

"How come?"

"Because you can't shoot for a passel of Mexican frijole beans and those old guns of yours might blow up in your face and hurt somebody."

"That ain't fair," Dillars said.

"It might not be, Rod, but I'm in charge here. You go on home."

Dillars hung his head and slunk off. Uberstrasse and

Millpas both snickered. Sheriff Keller breathed a sigh of relief.

Keller chose from among those who volunteered and seemed to have what he wanted, giving him eight men besides himself. Nine or ten ought to do it, he thought. He didn't know how good some of those he had chosen could shoot, but most of the men in town knew how to shoot a rifle and some were fair with a pistol, as well.

Just as he was about to give his final orders, Keller saw a man who had been standing off to the side all the time. He stayed after the others who had not been chosen had left.

"Sheriff," called the man. "I'm going with you."

"Who are you?"

"McKinney. Bill McKinney."

"Oh, yes, McKinney. Come on over here where I can see you."

McKinney walked over to the group of chosen men.

"Bill, I don't think it's a good idea that you come with us."

"That's my daughter, Ronnie, they took, Tom."

"I know, I know. But that's just the reason you ought to stay here and leave getting her back to us."

"What in hell are you talking about, Tom?"

"I mean, you got a bigger stake in this hunt than any of us. You might get trigger happy. You might shoot your own daughter."

"There's no damned chance of that," McKinney said, but Tom could see that he was still agitated and argumentative.

"We need cool heads here, Bill."

"Damn it, don't pussyfoot around me. I damned sure have a hell of a big stake in this. My daughter's the most important thing in my life."

"And that's just why I think you ought to stay out of this, Bill."

"No. I could never forgive myself if I didn't try with all

my heart and strength to rescue my daughter from those animals."

"You don't trust us?"

"Not with my daughter, I don't, Tom. It's nothing against you or these other good men here. But put yourself in my place. Just think of what you'd do if some bastards like these stole your only daughter."

"You've got a point, Bill," Keller admitted. "I just don't feel real good about you comin' along. You got big emotions and all. They might cloud your judgment when it gets down to closin' in on those murderers."

"I don't want revenge, Tom. I want my daughter back. That's all. And if I don't go with you, I'll go by myself."

"Aw, let him come," Millpas said. "He's got a bigger stake in getting those scoundrels than any of us."

"I agree, Tom," Uberstrasse said.

Roland and the others nodded in agreement.

The sheriff sighed and shrugged his shoulders. He knew that McKinney was a hothead and having his daughter taken away like that wouldn't help his temper any, but if he didn't let him come, Bill might go off on his own and make things worse.

"All right, Bill. You can come, but only on one condition."

"What's that?"

"I'm in charge. You do what I tell you. No goin' off on your own once we corner this bunch."

"I agree," McKinney said.

"All right. Now, go get your mounts, bring pistols, rifles, all the ammunition you've got, pick up your grub and meet me back here in, say, three quarters of an hour. Sooner, if you can."

The men all nodded assent and split up and left to get their horses, guns and ammunition. Keller mentally ticked off their names in his mind. Uberstrasse, Roland and Millpas, all crack shots. Robert Myers, a skilled hunter and woodsman, persistent as a bloodhound. Gordon Keith, a young buck with fire in his blood, but cool-headed. Bill Theodore, lean and thoughtful, sure and steady. Billy Brand, a muscular, keen-eyed woodsman who could drop a deer with a single shot, or bring down a turkey with a shot to the eye. Norman Lozier, another hunter, the best wing shot of the bunch. These were men he could count on. The only loose cannon in the bunch was McKinney. He would have to watch him real close.

"Be sure and fill your canteens," Keller called after them.

He turned to go back into his office. One of the men from the bank appeared from across the street and walked up to him.

"I hope you know what this is all about, Keller," the man said. His name was Harold Bowman. He was vice-president of the bank.

"I'll bring 'em back if I catch them," Keller said. "You weren't in the bank when it was robbed, were you?"

"No."

"Where were you?"

"I, uh, I was foreclosing on a loan out at the Eblen place."

"Then, you didn't see your friends getting murdered, did you, Harold?"

Bowman shifted the satchel in his hand and looked away for a moment.

"It's about the money they stole, Tom."

"No, it's not about the money, Harold. It's about Ronnie McKinney and the people those men killed."

"Just don't forget to bring back the money, Tom."

With that, Bowman walked away.

The sheriff watched him go and went inside his office, the anger building in him like a bomb fuse.

It is about the money, he thought. It's always about the money. Not just with bankers, but with most folks. But not with him. It was about that innocent girl and a bunch of murderers who had to be brought to justice.

He just hoped like hell he would be able to track them down and bring them back so that everyone could see them hang until they were dead.

And to hell with the bank, and Bowman and the money.

10

THEY RODE OUT OF THE STAND OF TREES AND JOBY SAW THE familiar beehives at the edges of the two fields dissected by the road to his parents' place. In the soft dirt of the road, he noticed the same tracks he had seen at his place. Shod horses had come in and out, leaving their marks in the dust, like signatures on a piece of paper.

He had committed them to memory by then, knowing he would need that information when he began to track ZP and the others. Tracking was something his father had first taught him and he had used some of that knowledge in the war.

When he was a boy, his father had made him lie flat on the ground and study a small square of grass and earth for hours at a time. At the end of that ordeal, he had to report to his father all that he had seen: the number of ants and doodlebugs he had witnessed crossing the patch of earth and grass, the way the grass dried in the sun or gave up its dew in the morning sun, the changes in soil as it dried or when it rained.

But his eyes were drawn to the house at the far end of

the road that was flanked by the two large fields of clover and lespedeza, fields empty of cattle or stock, fields that would yield hay at the end of summer—hay that he, Felicia and his sons would cut and haul to his place to store in the barn for winter.

"You've been tracking, haven't you, Joby?" Dolores asked.

"Some."

"You always did that when you were a boy."

"Habit, I guess."

"Except now it's important. Necessary, even."

"Yeah, maybe."

She did not talk anymore, nor did he, as they approached the house. Joby could almost feel the tension that was rising. The house, a small frame dwelling, sat very still and white. It looked deserted. It felt deserted. His mother might be doing the washing out back by the creek, or she could be sitting on the back porch in the shade. Except that he knew she wasn't. She didn't sit on the back porch in the middle of the day. She was a woman who kept busy, a person who thought that "idle hands were the devil's workshop."

No, Joby thought, something was wrong. Perhaps she was taking a nap, but as he looked up at the sun, he thought that it was too early. Rosalind took afternoon naps, never lay down in the morning.

"Joby," Dolores said, just before they reached the house.

"Yeah?"

"I'm worried. Ma's awful quiet. I don't see her."

"Let's not look for trouble, Sis."

"She would hear us coming, wouldn't she?"

"I don't know."

They stopped at the hitchrail that he had built at his mother's insistence. She said it showed a friendliness toward strangers to have a hitchrail outside the house. There was a little fence about knee high around the house. He and Do had put that up together about three years ago, a picket fence that his mother had painted white because she wanted to make it look nice.

Joby and Dolores dismounted and looped their reins loosely over the hitchrail. Dolores hung behind as Joby strode toward the front gate. He was about to go through the trellis, which was festooned with wisteria and ivy, when he stopped and looked back at his sister.

"You comin'?"

"Joby, I—I can't. Not right now. You go in and see if Ma's all right."

"I'll holler at you when I find her."

Joby went through the gate and up onto the porch. His boots made a hollow sound on the hardwood decking. The door to the front room was open, but the screen door was shut. And unlocked.

Joby stepped inside the front room and into a profound and eerie silence, the kind of silence that seemed to tick in his ears like a clock. He could hear his own breathing and it was loud as if he were the only one in the world who was alive.

"Ma?"

There was no answer and his voice echoed hollowly through the empty house. Joby drew in a breath and walked toward the kitchen at the back. The kitchen was empty. He called out his mother's name again.

Still no answer.

He walked back to the hall and down it to the bedrooms. He looked into Dolores's room and it was empty. His old room was the same. At the far end was where his mother slept, where his father had once gone to bed.

Joby opened the door to his parents' room and knew right away what he would find. He had smelled death before, and there was death in that room. He stepped inside, trying to quell the dread that filled his chest like a smothering essence, like smoke that he could not avoid.

Joby's mother lay on the opposite side of the bed, next to the wall. Her body was out of sight until he stepped clear over to that side of the bed. His heart sank when he saw her lying there, so still, so quiet. He felt a squeeze, as if someone's hand had taken his heart and clasped it so tight it stopped the blood.

He stood there for a moment, as if not wanting to verify that his mother was no longer breathing. But he could plainly see that she was not alive. She lay on her side, her head on one arm, the other stretched over her face as if to ward off another blow. Her face was partially hidden, facing downward at a three-quarter angle. But he could see the dark stain of clotted blood on the near side of her face and neck. There was blood spattered on the wall behind her, at just about the height she was. Whoever had forced her back into that corner and struck her must have wanted to look at her when he killed her.

Joby felt a queasiness in his stomach, a roiling of bile that threatened to double him up and make him retch. He drew a deep breath to ward off the sickness inside him and stepped around the bed and straddled his mother's body so that he could look at her face.

He reached down and tenderly moved her head so that he could see what had been done to her face. He winced when he saw the wound, the distorted features of her face.

Someone had struck his mother on the forehead. From the size and shape of the wound, it looked like she had been hit with the butt of a pistol. The killer had struck straight down with tremendous force, driving the pistol butt through her skull and into the front part of the brain.

There were dark bruises on his mother's throat and what

looked like hand or finger marks on her neck. So, whoever had struck her, had also strangled her.

"Ma, I'm sorry," Joby breathed, and it was like a prayer on his lips. He laid her head back down gently, glad that her eyes were already closed so that he did not have to do that. He reached up and pulled the coverlet from the bed and covered her body with the light quilt she had made with her own hands.

Joby got up and left the bedroom. He closed the door softly and walked back outside. Dolores was still standing by her horse at the hitchrail. He kept his head level, but even before he reached her, he knew that she knew.

"Do, she's gone," he said, and took his sister in his arms. He could feel her shaking long before he heard her sobs.

Then he started to cry, and they stood there, holding each other as they wept and comforted each other in a wordless embrace.

Before it was over, Joby felt the rage building inside him. He thought of ZP and the men with him. They had done this deliberately. They had done this to get even with him. Killed his mother, kidnapped his wife and raped his sister.

He knew that, somehow, way back in time, he had made a mistake, and now he was paying for it. He felt a terrible wave of guilt all of a sudden.

But underneath the guilt was a rage such as he had never felt before. He wanted to find those murderers and kill them with his bare hands, one by one. He wanted to make them suffer the pain he was feeling now. He wanted them to die real slow before he sent them straight to hell for eternity.

11

Tom Keller led the posse out of town in a procession, with he and Johnny Roland at the head of the column. A few people lined the streets and uttered cries of encouragement.

"Bring 'em back to hang, Tom."

"Get our money back, Sheriff."

"Hang 'em all, boys."

Keller ignored the people. He knew how easily they could become a mob if they smelled blood. He touched a finger to his hat, and that was all he gave to those who wanted his attention.

The column headed westward, following the tracks of the outlaws, tracks that were easy to see so soon after the robbery and killings.

"When we get well clear of town, Johnny," Keller said, "I want you to ride point and start tracking. You want anybody to go with you?"

"Millpas," Roland said. "He can keep a lookout for an ambush while I keep my eyes on the ground."

Keller made a noise with his lips and tongue that

showed his satisfaction. "Good thinking, Johnny. Do you think you'll have any trouble following their tracks?"

"Not right off. As long as they keep to the road. It's a matter of counting horses."

"What do you mean?"

"If one horse's tracks disappears, that could mean one of 'em doubled back to watch for a posse. That man could warn the main bunch and they could be waiting for us around the next bend, or in a clump of trees."

"Yeah, I see what you mean."

Once they left the gravity of Gilmet, the houses thinned out and then there were no more. Roland and Millpas separated from the rest of the posse and soon disappeared from sight. McKinney rode up front to ride alongside Sheriff Keller. The road wound lazily through woods and small patches of farmland. Most of the houses were set way back in the trees, but Keller knew there were not many people living this far from town. The folks who had settled the eastern part of Texas hid from marauding Apache, Comanche and Kiowa, not wanting to present easy targets for predatory red men.

"How far do you think that bunch is ahead of us, Tom?" McKinney asked.

"Hard to tell. I'm not a tracker, like Johnny, but they don't seem to be in any particular hurry. Next place we'll come to is Redmond's. He's passed on, but his widder and daughter still live on the old place."

"That's Joby's kin."

"Sister and mother."

"Well, they probably don't have nothin' to worry about. Those bastards got what they wanted in town."

"Hard to tell," Keller said.

He didn't want to voice his fears to McKinney, who was wound up tight as a watch spring. He wished the man would not ride up front with him, but he let it go for the time being. The robbers just might want to take more hostages, and an old lady and a young girl wouldn't be that hard to overcome and kidnap. But he said nothing about this possibility. And, as it turned out, he didn't have to. A half hour later, he saw Roland and Millpas riding toward them. Both were in a hurry.

"Uh-oh," McKinney said. "They found something."

Keller said nothing. He waited until the two men rode up, and waited for Roland to report.

"Tom, we found some puzzlin' tracks up ahead."

"How so?"

"A mix of old and new. Same horses. Different ages to the tracks."

"What in hell does that mean?" Keller asked.

"I'll show you," Roland said. "But Bob and I follered the tracks, the fresh ones, goin' into the woods."

"And we found something," Millpas said.

"What?" Keller asked.

Millpas's mouth flickered with a lazy smile.

"Come see," Roland said. "They had a camp here. Long before they come to Gilmet."

"What?"

Roland and Millpas nodded.

"We'd better take a look," Keller said.

"Foller me," Roland said. He and Millpas set out and the column, headed by Keller and McKinney, trailed close behind them. A ripple of excitement spread through the members of the posse.

Keller was chewing on the information Millpas and Roland had given him. Keller had thought, like most everyone else in town, that the criminals had just ridden into town from the south and west, possibly after escaping from the prison in Huntsville, with the intention of robbing the bank. If they had been in the area for some time before they rode into town, he wondered why, and he wondered what they might have been doing. How long had the gang been hiding out in the woods?

Roland and Millpas stopped where the fresh tracks left the road. Roland pointed down to the ground, showing Sheriff Keller the maze of tracks.

"Me'n Bob figger that bunch came here first after they left Gilmet," Roland said. "And, soon's you see their camp, you'll know we were right."

"Lead on, Johnny," Keller said.

Apparently, the robbers had found an old game trail and followed it into the woods. Roland led the posse to a small clearing deep in the pines, with plenty of small trees all around, and brush, for concealment. The killers had chosen the spot well.

"Well, I'll be damned," Keller said, when he saw the spot that Millpas and Roland had pointed out to him. There were, indeed, signs that the outlaws had stayed there for some time.

"It sure does stink here," Brand said, his nose crinkling in revulsion.

The campsite was strewn with empty whiskey bottles, discarded airtights, empty sacks of coffee, beans, flour and sugar. There was a pair of worn-out boots with holes in their soles, pieces of leather straps, a faded saddle blanket, old socks, a bandanna or two and many limp sacks of makings tossed all around.

"They been here a while," Keller said.

"And they were busy when they were here," Millpas said. "They wore trails from here through the woods to the west. A lot of comin' and goin'."

"Looks to me like they was scoutin'," Roland said. "The Redmond place lies yonder through them woods. Where the widder and her daughter live."

Keller looked the camp over carefully. He rode over to a

thick copse of trees. The trees were set close together, with low-hanging branches. Below the limbs, on the ground, there was a fire ring, rocks set in a circle. The rocks were blackened from fire and smoke. The ground inside the circle of rocks was full of ashes.

"They made their cookfire here, so the smoke would break up in the trees," Keller said. "They didn't want anyone to know they were here."

"Looks that way," said Uberstrasse, who had ridden over to examine the site. "They were real careful."

Keller turned his horse and rode back to talk to Roland and Millpas. They were both rolling smokes. Millpas had his leg up on the cantle, the calf wrapped around the saddle horn for support.

"How long do you figure they stayed here, Johnny?" Keller asked.

Roland licked the cigarette paper, sealing it around the tobacco. He stuck the cigarette into one side of his mouth.

"I puzzled over that when we come up here, Tom. Bob and I talked about it some."

"And what did you think?"

"Bob said two weeks. I figger more like three weeks to a month."

"That long?" Keller asked.

"Just lookin' at the trash heap will give you some idea, and the way the ground is stirred up. Lots of comings and goings."

"I agree," Millpas said. "I lost count of the cigarette butts ground into the soil with their boot heels, and that smell comes from a hole they dug over yonder, 'bout a hunnert yards away. They lived here."

"Close to town," Keller said. "But closer to something else, I figure."

"Closer to someone, maybe," Norm Lozier piped up. "The widder woman and her daughter, maybe."

"You've got a point, Norm," Keller said. "Why don't you and Billy Brand follow that trail through the woods and see where it goes, what they did. Make it quick. Every minute we spend here jawin', those boys are puttin' distance 'twixt us and them."

"Let's go, Billy," Lozier said, riding off. The most worn path away from the camp led into the woods to the west, and the two men took it, riding at a half-gallop.

"That's a good idea, Tom," Roland said. "Me 'n Bob wanted to ride through there, too. They made a hell of a big rut thataway whilst they was here."

"That's what worries me," Keller said. "Those boys were up to a lot more than robbin' the bank in Gilmet and killin' those folks."

"What do you mean?"

"We know they had help robbin' the bank. Maybe somebody else around here gave 'em some help, too."

"Huh?" Millpas said. "You mean, they was in cahoots with folks who live out here?"

"You're not talking about Joby Redmond, are you, Tom?" Roland asked.

The sheriff heaved a sigh, but said nothing.

But that was exactly what he was thinking right then.

12

DOLORES LISTENED TO THE HAMMER BLOWS AND SHOOK WITH every strike that drove nails in her mother's coffin. Joby was out in the barn, building a casket for her, just as he had done for their father. She looked at the body of her mother lying on the bed and was gripped with a deep sadness.

She had washed her mother's body and now was ready to finish dressing her. She had laid out her mother's favorite dress, a simple dress the woman had bought in Gilmet, a print dress with yellow and blue flowers. She slipped the dress gently over her mother's head, worked her stiff arms through the sleeves then smoothed it out. She had put a touch of rouge on her mother's cheeks and lips, but it hadn't helped.

Tears coursed down Do's cheeks as she looked again at her mother's face, so still, so rigid, so mirthless in death. Rosalind's eyes were closed and she would have looked as if she had been sleeping, were it not for the wound on her forehead. Do had powdered her mother's neck to try and hide the bruise marks, but she could still see their shadows beneath the fragrant powder.

"Oh, Ma," Dolores said, wiping away some of the tears from beneath her eyes. "I love you so."

The hammering continued as Dolores put stockings on her mother's legs, and finally worked on the shoes, black ones that she wore to church, that were always kept shined. She smelled the lilac fragrance she had splashed on her mother's cheeks and behind her ears. Then she pulled her mother's arms down and folded her hands over her heart.

Dolores stepped back and surveyed her mother's appearance. If she closed her eyes slightly, it appeared her mother was only asleep, but she knew she was dead. Joby had tried to shield her from the worst, but when she bathed her mother's body, she knew more than he did. Her killer had punched her and there were bruises on her abdomen and on her breasts. Those ugly dark marks on her mother's skin had made her cringe when she first saw them.

The hammering stopped suddenly and Dolores felt a twinge of fear. If Joby had finished building the casket for their mother, then they'd soon have to put her in the ground, say their final farewells. Dolores was engulfed with another wave of deep sadness at the thought that she would never see her mother again. There would always be that hole in her life, that empty place where her mother had always been, and now was no more.

She heard a clatter on the porch a few minutes later and then a heavy hollow sound as wood struck wood. She knew that Joby had brought the casket up to the house. When they had buried their father, their mother had insisted that there be enough pine lumber leftover to make her own casket. In fact, she had wanted Joby to build it right away, but he had refused.

"You're going to be with us a long time, Ma," he had said. "You don't have to worry about having a casket ready for you."

Their mother had shaken her head.

"I thought Pa would be here a long time, too," she said. "We all have to prepare for our final moments on this earth."

Still, Dolores thought, death was always an unexpected event. There was no way to prepare for the loss of a loved one, especially a parent. She had always thought her parents would be alive forever, as long as she was.

Joby appeared in the doorway of the bedroom. He had walked into the house so softly she had not heard him. He carried a long wide and thin board, which he leaned against the wall, just inside the door.

He had his hat in his hand, out of respect. He had taken it off just before entering the room.

"You did a good job, Do," he said, looking at their mother. "She—she looks nice in that dress."

"It was her favorite." Do wiped away the tears. There were dark streaks on her face and when Joby looked at her, he saw that she no longer seemed like a little girl. There was an oldness in her eyes that had not been there before, as if her youth had fled and she was now looking out at the world not from a child's perspective, but with the eyes of a woman, a woman who had seen too much of life.

"I want to play some music at her grave," Dolores said. "I want to sing a couple of her favorite songs when we bury her."

"I think she would like that, Do." There was a huskiness in his voice, a rasp that seemed to be born of strong emotion. "We have to carry her out to the porch and then put the, ah, casket, on the handcart. I can wheel it out to the grave while you get your dulcymore."

"Wouldn't it have been better to leave the casket on the cart?"

"Too wobbly. I want Ma to rest comfortably."

"I understand," she said.

Joby had dug the grave already and had measured his

mother, but he wasn't sure if she would fit in the casket. He didn't want to risk dropping her, or having the casket slide off the cart while he was putting her inside the pine box. But he didn't tell Dolores of his fears.

"Maybe we ought to say a prayer for her first," Joby said. "Before we move her."

"You say it, Joby."

Joby stepped up close to the bed and looked down at his mother's face. He closed his eyes and spoke just above a whisper.

"Lord, we pray you take our mother in your arms and keep her safe. Give her to our father so that he may love her again like he did when he was down here with her. Thank you, Lord, for all your blessings. Amen."

Dolores started sobbing again. "That was real nice, Joby."

Joby let out a long sigh and opened his eyes. He wished he did not have to see his mother like this. It was not the way he wanted to remember her. He wanted to think of her laughing and singing when Do played the dulcimer. He wanted to think of her face lit by sunshine and her hair pulled back in a bun, her eyes all shining and happy when she was out in the garden. He wanted to think of her at the supper table, passing the food and smiling at them with love in her heart.

"I'll get the board," Joby said. "You can help me slide it under her."

"Be careful, Joby. We don't want to hurt her."

Joby looked at her, then walked over to the wall and got the board. He brought it back to the bed and lay it beside his mother.

"That was dumb of me to say that," she said.

"No, it wasn't, Do. It feels like she's still with us."

"I know. It does, doesn't it?"

"I think she is. She's lookin' down at us."

He slid his hand under his mother's shoulder and lifted her, sliding the board underneath with his other hand. He and Dolores worked their way down to her feet, gently lifting one side of her body and pushing the board underneath.

"Now, we'll pull her toward us until she's all the way on the board, Do."

"All right."

They got the board completely underneath their mother. Both were puffing some from exertion.

"You take her feet, Do. I'll go out first, backward."

The two took their positions, each grabbing the sides of the board at either end. Joby nodded when he saw that Dolores was ready and they lifted the body of their mother. Joby was surprised at how light she was. He backed out through the door and down the hall, with Dolores following. He pushed the front door open with his buttocks and they went onto the porch.

"Just set your end on the side of the casket, Do. I'll take it from there. Make sure it's on solid."

Dolores nodded and set down her end. "Where's the lid to the coffin?" she asked.

"I took it out to the grave. I'll nail it on after we get over there."

It took him a few minutes to position his mother and then he asked Dolores to lift her feet and slide her end of the board away. He put his hands and arms under his mother's shoulder blades. Together they lowered their mother into the casket.

"She fits," Joby said, as if surprised.

"I want to put something of hers in it with her, Joby."

"Go get it. Those men are putting more distance between us with every minute we stay here."

"This is important," Dolores snapped.

"I didn't mean it that way, hon."

"I'll be right back."

Dolores returned a few moments later with a small coin purse that belonged to her mother. She opened it and showed Joby what was inside. There was a penny, a silver dollar and a five-dollar gold piece.

"She won't need that money," Joby said, wanting to bite his tongue even after he had uttered the words.

"This was money Ma put aside for a rainy day, as she put it. I think this is that day, Joby."

"You're right. Ma will like that, I think."

Dolores closed the purse and placed it next to her mother. She straightened her dress and patted her hair.

"I'm ready," she said.

"You take the feet end and I'll back down the porch. We'll just slide the casket onto the cart."

When they had finished placing the casket on the cart, Joby got ready to push it.

"I'll go get the dulcymore and meet you out there," she said. "Unless you need help pushing the cart."

"No, I'll get it."

As Dolores climbed back up the steps and entered the house again, Joby began to push the cart away. There was a small hill north of the house that his father had set aside for the family burial plot. It was surrounded by live oaks and some leafy box elders he had planted. It was shady there and grassy, quiet.

The cart creaked and to Joby it sounded like a mournful funeral dirge. He looked at his mother and the tears flowed again. He didn't bother wiping them away.

"Yes, Ma," he muttered to himself. "I guess this is that rainy day."

And he felt something squeezing his heart when he got to the burial place, and he knew it was the beginning of a grief that would last for some while, perhaps his entire lifetime. He took off his hat and wiped the sweat from his forehead.

That's when he saw movement in the trees off to his left as he was looking down at the house, seeing Dolores come through the front door. He turned and stared straight into the place where he had seen the movement and he felt his heart skip a beat.

Someone was there, he knew. Someone was watching them. And he himself was unarmed. He held his breath. Then, as he started to wave at Dolores to send her back to the house, he heard someone call out from the trees.

It was a man's voice and it was calling his name.

13

Two men rode out of the trees, heading toward the burial ground on the little hill.

"Joby, we're ridin' up," Billy Brand called. "Me 'n Norm."

"Come ahead," Joby called, startled that two men he knew from town would be riding up at this time.

Dolores started to run. She was carrying the dulcimer in its little sack. The heavy canvas sack was slung over her shoulder. Joby beckoned to her, reassuring her that it was all right.

The two men and Dolores all arrived at the grove of shade trees at about the same time.

"Joby, what happened? Is that your ma in there?" Brand asked.

Joby nodded.

"How'd she die?" Lozier asked, as both men removed their hats out of respect.

"She was murdered," Dolores said.

Joby looked at her, surprised at the anger in her voice.

"What brings you boys out thisaway?" Joby asked.

"We're part of the posse from Gilmet. A bunch of men robbed the bank and killed some folks. Sheriff Keller's on the hunt for 'em."

"Those killers have been watchin' your folks' place here, Joby," Lozier said. "For about a month. We rode over here from their camp to see what they were a-lookin' at."

"Well, I don't know why they'd want to kill my mother, but they did," Joby said. And they've been to my place already. Took my wife, Felicia, with them. You better ride on back and bring Tom and the others over here. I'm going after those bastards soon's I bury my ma."

"They aren't far away, just on the other side of that little patch of woods yonder," Brand said. "Won't take us long to bring 'em all here. If you don't mind, we'd all be obliged to pay our respects."

"You better get to it, then," Joby said. "We're goin' ahead with the buryin'. Those killers are burnin' daylight."

"Be right back," Lozier said, and the two men turned their horses and galloped off, back the way they had come.

"They broke the spell," Dolores said.

"Yeah. But, they're part of a posse. We could sure use some help. We're goin' up against some pretty rough old boys."

Dolores pouted and lay her canvas bag with the dulcimer in it under a tree. Joby could see that she was still angry over the unexpected intrusion. He didn't like it any more than she did. He didn't know how far away Sheriff Keller and the others were, but if he hurried, he might get their mother buried before they showed up.

He looked at the pile of dirt next to the grave, and beyond it, to the sod he had saved to put back over the dirt that would cover his mother's coffin. He had used a spade to cut the grass into squares, then dug deep enough to preserve the grass roots. He had stacked the sod in the shade of an oak tree. There would be a lot of work to do after he and Dolores lowered the casket into the ground.

"I'll nail that lid on the coffin, Sis. Why don't you break out your dulcymore and get it tuned up."

"I don't feel like playin' now," she said, her face dark with the sullen mood she was in, as if a cloud had passed over the sun and left her in shadow.

"Suit yourself," he said. "But you said you were goin' to play for Ma."

He turned his back on her then, and picked up the lid of the coffin, set it in place. He walked over to one of the trees and picked up a can of nails and a hammer. By the time he drove in the first nail, Dolores was sitting down and untying the strings that held the canvas bag closed. Their mother had sewn the dulcimer case for her and decorated it with bluebonnet petals she had made from cloth she dyed. His mother was always doing things like that for him and his sister, and it was hard to imagine that she would do them no more.

"Do you need a chair to sit on?" Joby asked, as Dolores pulled the dulcimer from its bag.

"No, I'll just sit on the ground, close to Ma's grave."

"I'm going to need help getting this casket in the grave."

"I'll help." She rose up from the ground, leaving her dulcimer atop its canvas sack and walked over to the casket.

"I brought some rope," he said. "I'll slip the rope around the front of the box. Then we can put the casket at one end of the grave and slide it forward. I'll hold on to the rope around the end going in first to guide it, if you can push it, real slow, straight ahead. Then I should be able to lower my end gently and bring the rope to your end and do the same thing."

"I can do that," she said, glancing at the puddle of rope over by the shovel that was leaning against one of the box elders.

"All right. Let me push the cart into position."

Joby pulled the cart away from the grave, backing it up. Then he headed straight for the grave, stopping the length of the casket short of the hole he had dug.

"That ought to do it," he said. "Now, you grab the other end while I slide the cart out from under. Just keep it from falling hard, Do. You don't have to take the full weight of it."

"I understand."

"First, I'll lay the rope down so's it'll be under the casket when we get ready to move it to the grave."

Joby went over and picked up the rope. He lay it parallel to the grave, just at the edge. As he walked back to the cart to begin sliding the coffin off it and onto the ground, Dolores lifted her hand.

"What is it?" he asked.

"I hear something," she said.

Joby listened. He heard it, too.

"Horses," he said. "Riding through the woods yonder. Must be the posse comin'."

"Maybe we'd better wait, Joby. They can help us lower Ma's coffin into the ground."

"I was hopin' we'd be finished before they got back."

"They must not have gone far, those two who were here."

"No, and that gives me a crawly feelin'."

"Huh?"

"To know that ZP and those others were so close."

"Watching us, maybe," she said.

"Maybe. Probably."

Dolores and Joby waited, the sound of hoofbeats growing louder in their ears. Soon they saw the riders emerging from the piney woods, all at a gallop, all heading their way at a fair clip.

"That's Sheriff Keller," Dolores said. "And Ronnie's father's with him."

"That's quite a posse," Joby said. "And they look like they mean business."

"Well, they'd better," Dolores spat. "I hope they kill every one of those bastards."

"Take it easy, Sis. Worst thing you can do is show your temper right now."

"Why?"

"Those men there could turn into a bloodthirsty mob right quick."

"I see what you mean. I only know Ronnie's father, Mr. McKinney. I've seen Sheriff Keller in town, but I don't know him. Ma didn't like him."

"Well, just hold your tongue while they're here. Keep in mind they came here to help us."

"I will," she said, but Joby noticed there was still a frown on her face.

Joby looked at the riders again. They had brought no pack horses, he noticed, and that meant that Keller had hoped to catch up to Popper and his gang in a few hours. If so, he was in for a big surprise. Joby had tracked Popper and his bunch before. They knew how to travel and if he had to guess, he'd bet ZP had fresh horses waiting for him somewhere along his trail. This sure as hell wasn't going to be a one- or two-day job.

He breathed deeply, and waited for the men to come up. He had already made up his mind to leave his boys at home. He didn't want to put them in danger, and he had a strong hunch that he was going to end up going after Popper all by himself.

That posse had little stake in the fate of Felicia and Veronica McKinney. And, he sure as hell wasn't going to take a tenderfoot like Bill McKinney along on a dangerous hunt like this one.

Suddenly, his task seemed a hopeless one, and if he had not had enough trouble and grief with Dolores, and his mother and Felicia, it looked to him as if more was sure as hell riding his way.

Oh, they meant well, Joby knew, but they didn't know the men they were hunting.

Joby did know them, and he dreaded the long, uncertain days that were surely to come.

14

SHERIFF TOM KELLER ASSESSED THE SITUATION QUICKLY.

"Real sorry about your ma, Joby. We'll lend a hand with that casket there."

"Obliged," Joby said. "Light down, all of you."

The men in the posse all nodded and rode to places where they could hitch their horses to bushes and trees. In moments, they were all around the gravesite. Keller and Uberstrasse slapped Joby on the back, while others murmured their condolences.

Joby looked at the faces of the men who had come, nodding to each one. He knew them all, knew some had given up time away from their farms and families.

"If you could lend a hand," Joby said, "this won't take long. Do's going to sing some and play her dulcymore and I'll say a few words over my ma's grave."

"That's fine, Joby, just fine," Keller said. "Tommy, Johnny, you take that far end. Joby and I will take up the rope on this end."

The act of helping out and putting hands to task seemed

to take a lot of the tension out of the group, and that included Joby and Dolores. The casket was lowered into the ground without incident, and the ropes withdrawn and laid aside.

"Much obliged for your help," Joby said to Keller and the others.

They all nodded without speaking.

Joby turned to his sister. "Dolores, do you want to get your dulcymore?"

She nodded and left to get her instrument. The possemen and the sheriff all removed their hats and stood at graveside in reverent attitudes as Dolores returned with the dulcimer. She sat beneath a large box elder next to her mother's open grave and placed the dulcimer on her lap.

Joby took off his hat and looked over at his sister.

"Our ma loved to hear the dulcymore," Dolores said. "She played it herself and taught me. She brought it all the way out from Kentucky. I'm singin' these songs for our ma and she's likely helpin' me play."

There were four strings on the dulcimer, two set close together and tuned to the same note in the treble clef, one octave above the string tuned to the bass clef. The frets were made with horseshoe nails, the body of the instrument was curly maple, and the top made from cherry wood. Dolores bowed her head and drew in a breath. Then she began to play, strumming the instrument with her right hand while her fingers pressed on the strings that were across the frets.

She first sang "Rosewood Casket," then she played an old hymn, "Swing Low, Sweet Chariot." Her fingers flew over the frets and the music that poured forth was sweet and mellow. Her voice was in perfect harmony with the melodies and the blend of voice and music was almost celestial. Finally, she lifted her head to the sky for a moment, then began to play and sing "Wayfarin' Stranger." When she voiced the words, "I'm goin' home to see my mother," some of the men shed a tear.

"She liked "Greensleeves" a lot, too," Dolores said, "but I'll sing that to her another time. I love you, Ma."

Joby heaved a sigh and stepped up to the open grave and looked down into it. His sister bowed her head and so did the men standing solemnly nearby.

"Lord," Joby intoned, "we pray that You keep our mother safe in heaven and fill her soul with Your loving grace. She was a good woman and she taught us Your Word and the Golden Rule. Good-bye, Ma, and may you rest eternally in peace."

"Amen," Dolores said, and the men all murmured, "Amen."

"Amen," Joby said, and choked back the urge to weep. His eyes filled with sudden tears. Dolores set her dulcimer down and rose from the ground. She walked over to her brother and put her arms around his chest and hugged him tightly. He embraced her, as well, and they stood there until their quiet sobbing was under control.

"I love you, Sis," Joby whispered.

"Oh, Joby," she said. "I love you, too."

Then they broke from each other. Joby wiped his eyes as his sister walked over and picked up her dulcimer, and put it back in its sack.

Joby walked over and picked up the shovel, then strode back to the open grave.

"I've only got one shovel," he said, as he began to scoop the loose soil from the top of the mound.

"We'll spell you," Roland said.

"Right," Keller said, as if wary that Roland was usurping some of his authority.

"It won't take long," Joby said. "I guess you boys are after that bunch because of Bill McKinney's daughter."

"They robbed the bank, too," Gordon Keith said.

"And they kilt Lou Marshall," Bill Theodore said.

"Two more besides them," Norm Lozier put in. "The bank manager, Bert Loomis, and the head clerk, Elmer Reynolds."

"Reynolds?" Joby said, pausing his empty shovel in midair.

"Somebody at the bank said he was in cahoots with the robbers," Keith said. "Said he used to be a guard down at Huntsville."

Joby felt a twinge rip through his heart. His face went ashen for a moment. Keller noticed it and walked over, put his hand on the handle of the shovel.

"You know anything about this, Redmond?" Keller asked.

"We had a Reynolds in Company K, Second Texas," he said. "But he didn't desert like Popper and the others."

"Are you sure?"

"Dead sure," Joby said. "I didn't know he was thick with Popper."

"Is Popper someone you know? And was he one of those who took your wife?"

"I'm sure of it. Yes, I knew him. And his bunch. Bad, every one of 'em, bad to the bone."

Keller released his grip on the shovel handle and stepped back. There was a deep silence among the men. They all stared at Joby Redmond as if he had just turned into a large bug.

Joby would never have suspected Reynolds to be in cahoots with Popper. But now that he looked back on it, he began to remember little things. Reynolds and Botts had been pretty thick during the campaigns. And Botts was a coward and a schemer.

"Just how much do you know about these fellers?" Keller asked.

"They were deserters," Joby said. "I tracked them

down. They were all sent away to Huntsville for crimes they committed after they deserted. They should still be in prison, as far as I'm concerned."

"They should be hanged," McKinney said. "And I'd like to be the one who shakes out the rope."

Joby scowled. He scooped up another clump of dirt and threw it down into the hole. This posse, he decided, was going to be trouble. He didn't know how strong a man Sheriff Keller was, but if he didn't watch his step, the men following him would just turn out to be another lynch party.

"Well," Joby said, panting from the exertion, "the first order of business is to catch them, and knowing what I know about Ezekiel Popper and his bunch, that's not going to be easy. He's had a lot of practice in avoiding the law."

"You caught him, didn't you?" McKinney asked.

Joby looked at him, trying to hide his disgust.

"It took a while," he said.

"Then we'd better get going after them," McKinney said.

Nobody said anything. Then McKinney coughed and looked embarrassed.

"I mean after you finish burying your dear mother, Joby."

"One of you men spell Joby here," Keller said. "He's right. We'll go after the killers as soon as this business here is finished."

Joby shot Keller a look of gratitude.

Perhaps, he thought, Keller was a leader. He wondered, though, if Keller realized that he had a big liability with Bill McKinney.

McKinney wanted blood, and unless the sheriff had a strong leash on him, he could spoil everything. In fact, he reasoned, McKinney shouldn't even be a member of the posse. He was a loose cannon rolling around on the deck of a pitching ship.

Tommy Uberstrasse stepped forward and took the shovel from Joby.

"Let me do it some," Tommy said. "You done enough."

"Thanks," Joby said, handing him the shovel.

Some of the men broke out the makings and built smokes. McKinney took out a cigar and bit off the end of it. He reached into his pocket and took out another one and handed it to the sheriff. Keller took the cigar and Joby thought about that for a while.

McKinney was buttering up Keller, and he put Keller at fault for allowing that small bribe.

But Joby realized that now was not the time to bring up the issue of taking McKinney along on the hunt for Popper and the others.

There would come a time, he was sure, and he meant to speak up about it. In no uncertain terms.

McKinney did not offer Joby a cigar and Joby was glad. It allowed him to hide his feelings about McKinney a while longer.

Within a half hour, the grave was finished, the dirt piled high and smoothed off, rounded, the sod put back on top of the fresh dirt.

Joby looked around for Dolores, but he didn't see her. She must have gone back to the house, he figured.

"I'll stop and get my horse, say good-bye to my sister," Joby told Keller. "Then we can ride to my place and I'll pick up another mount to bring, and some grub."

"What about your boys?" Keller asked.

"I've decided to leave them at home, to look after my sister. I'll be going with you."

The sheriff looked relieved. "That'd be mighty fine. I could use your experience, Joby."

"Did you say your sister was a-stayin' here?" Roland asked, looking at Joby.

"Yeah, sure. Why?"

"'Cause, less'n I'm mistaken, she's a-settin' on her horse and got yours by the reins, a-waitin' for you. And she's got that stringed box slung over her shoulder."

Joby looked down toward the house.

Roland was right. Dolores was sitting her horse, and she had a bedroll tied in back of the cantle of her saddle, and saddlebags that appeared to be bulging.

"I'll take care of it," Joby said.

As the others caught up their horses, Joby walked down toward the house. He didn't know what his sister had in mind, but she sure as hell wasn't going to ride with him and this posse.

Not if he had anything to say about it.

15

JOBY WAS MORE PUZZLED THAN ANGRY. GRIEF, HE REASONED, sometimes made people do strange things, and he was sure that his sister was no exception. She had been closer to, and more dependent on, their mother than he had been, so he was thinking that she was more stricken than he was. Burying a loved one, a parent or a child, was a difficult burden to bear.

So, when Joby walked up to Dolores, he was struggling with a thicket-full of tangled feelings. Especially, when she held out her hand to give him the reins to his horse, as if they were just going on a Sunday ride through the country.

She had changed her clothes, too, and was wearing a pair of coveralls and her work boots, a calico shirt, and a wide-brimmed hat. She had a red bandanna around her neck, as well.

"Where do you think you're going?" Joby asked.

"With you. After those men. After the man who raped me, and after the one who came back in the house and killed our ma."

Joby did not take the reins from her. Instead, he stood

there, feet wide apart in the stance of a man with absolute authority.

"Do, you don't know what you'd be getting into. This isn't a hayride or a picnic. These are very dangerous men."

"I know that. I can shoot, you know that. You and Pa taught me."

"You think those men are just going to line up like empty airtights so's you can pick them off, one by one?"

"No. I've shot running deer, and plugged turkeys through the eye."

"This isn't the same thing."

"I know it isn't. Joby, don't fight me on this. I've made up my mind."

"Do, I can't take you with me. It just wouldn't be right. Too dangerous."

"You're taking Forrest and Mark."

"No, I'm not," he said.

"They think you are."

"I know. I'm going to tell them they have to stay behind and look after you."

Her eyes flared with anger, and Joby could almost feel the heat from her as the hand with the rein in it shook the tailing leather end at him.

"I don't need lookin' after, Joby. And, those boys are dead set on goin' along with you. You can't break their hearts this way. You can't break my heart like this. We want to help. We want to be with you. Wherever you go."

Joby was not prepared for Dolores's outburst. He'd had no idea that her feelings ran so deep. When that man had violated her, he probably sparked some ferocity in her that was unintended. The sister who spoke to him now was not the sister he had known all his life, not the girl he had grown up with, then left behind when he went to war. Nor was she the sister he had met when he returned home.

"Well," he said, "I'm not taking the boys with me. And

if I think this is too much for you, wherever we might be on the trail, I'll send you back home. Is that clear?"

"I won't be any trouble," she said, shaking the tail end of his reins at him. "As you said before, time's a-wastin'. Let's go."

Joby resisted the urge to jerk the reins from her hand and pull her from her horse. He had to bite his tongue to keep from venting more of his feelings about her coming along, but he held it all back. He would keep an eye on her, and if he thought she was going to be in the way, or get hurt, he'd send her packing, back home.

He took the reins from Dolores and walked around, giving her a last glaring look before he mounted his horse. The posse, who had been waiting at the road leading off the property, put their horses in motion when he and Dolores came close.

Joby rode up to the head of the column to talk to Keller. McKinney was riding alongside him, further adding to Joby's misgivings about the entire expedition.

"You aim to bring your sister along, Redmond?" Keller asked.

"Try and stop her, Tom."

"If she . . ."

"Don't worry," Joby said. "I've already talked to her. She knows the situation and the conditions I've set."

"I don't like it none," Keller said.

"Neither do I. But, that's the way it is."

"I'm sorry your wife got taken," Keller said. "Johnny told me. It must be tough."

"Felicia's a strong woman."

"That's a vicious bunch. There was no reason for them to kill those people in Gilmet. But you know them better'n I do."

"Ezekiel Popper likes to watch people die. That whole bunch is bloodthirsty."

"So, you had dealings with them," Keller said.

"They were deserters. I had to track them down."

"How did you catch them?"

"It took me a while. I kept the pressure up on them, learned their habits, figured out where they were going next and then slacked off."

"Slacked off? You mean you stopped chasing them?"

"Something like that. I wanted them to think I had given up on them. I knew they were running low on supplies, were out of money, and wanted female company."

"So, what did you do?"

"I rode on ahead of them to the next place I figured they'd go to, and staked out the bank and general store. I had telegraphed my outfit and several soldiers met me there. It was a little town called Vickery, over by Dallas."

"Never heard of it."

"One of the outlaws was from there, Pete Hayes. I figured ZP would go there. There really wasn't a bank there, but there was a place where people took their money for safekeeping. Town was small enough, I could cover it with a couple of squads. They were all dressed in women's clothes."

Keller loosed a short, harsh laugh.

"You dressed troops up like women?"

"Vickery looked like the Easter Parade the day Popper, Hayes, Richardson, Botts, and Duggan rode in, hungry as wolves, horny as yearling bulls, and broke as privates at the end of the month."

"So, did they put up a fight?"

"There was some lead slung," Joby said. "But, I think they got rattled when all those 'ladies' started rushing them, holding big six-guns, Spencer repeating rifles, and a Gatling gun chewing up wood on a building right behind them. They shot one of my men and Duggan was slightly wounded. They threw up their hands and tossed down their iron right quick when they saw all these 'women' coming at them like the witches of hell."

Keller laughed aloud then. McKinney scowled, as if he didn't get the humor of the situation. Joby noticed that.

"That was mighty smart thinking," Keller said.

"It took me months to get that smart. Make no mistake, Popper is dangerous, and he learned a lot from me hunting him. He won't make the same mistake again."

"I reckon people like Popper was just plumb born bad."

"I learned some things about him when those boys went to trial," Joby said.

"Like what?"

"Before the war, Popper and Duggan killed two families, ranchers that lived as neighbors. Popper took over one place, and Duggan the other. Like squatters. Only they murdered folks for the land."

"Lord Jesus," Keller said. "You don't mean it."

Joby shrugged. "Those two were just born mean. And hard-hearted. Gilmet got off lucky, if you get right down to it."

"Lucky?"

"If we don't put those boys back in prison, or stretch their necks, they'll likely kill a whole town someday and just take it over, pretty as you damned please."

Even Keller shuddered. Joby looked at McKinney. His face had blanched until he looked like a man who had never seen the sun.

"You don't need to talk about such, Redmond," McKinney said. "You know they got my daughter. I don't need remindin' of how coldhearted and mean they are."

"Sorry, McKinney," Joby said. "But I wasn't just spoutin' gossip. I was recitin' chapter and verse about Zeke Popper and that bunch."

"Well, I've had a damned bellyful," McKinney said, and turned his horse away to fall behind Keller and Joby.

They were approaching Joby's place, and they all smelled smoke and a stench that made them wrinkle their noses.

"What's that?" Keller asked.

"Oh, didn't I tell you, Tom?" Joby said. "Popper tried to kill all my horses, and he did kill a few of them. I expect my sons have dragged the dead ones into a pile and are burning them."

McKinney gagged and Joby thought he was going to throw up. The stench was stronger the closer they got to the ranch. Finally, McKinney leaned over in the saddle and retched. Vomit spewed from his mouth and his body convulsed from the contractions.

"Drink you some water from that canteen of yours, Bill," Keller said.

McKinney vomited again.

"You're going to smell worse than them horses," said Roland, who was riding right behind them. "Just don't get any of that shit on me."

McKinney was voiceless, gripped now with the dry heaves.

"What'd you bring him along for, Tom?" Joby asked Keller. "He's not fit for a job like this."

"I couldn't keep him from comin', Joby. The man had blood in his eye."

"Well, if he's not careful, he's liable to wind up with no blood at all."

Keller said nothing, but when Joby looked at the sheriff, he could see that the man was thinking. Thinking real hard.

16

Joby's sons, Mark and Forrest, stood outside the house and pulled their bandannas down from their faces to reveal their mouths agape at the mass of men and their aunt Dolores riding up on them.

"I want to talk to my boys in private, Tom," Joby told Keller.

"It looks like they're ready to ride, Joby. Horses saddled, a little remuda roped up to bring along."

"That reminds me of something I meant to ask you, Tom."

"What's that?"

"How long did you intend to chase after those long riders?"

"A couple of days. Why?"

"You didn't bring any spare horses. These boys will wear yours plumb out in a week."

"It won't take us that long to tree those killers."

Joby suppressed a mocking laugh.

"I wish I had your confidence."

"They only have a few hours head start on us. They got to rest. They don't have no extra mounts."

"I figure they do," Joby said.

"They didn't when they left Gilmet."

"No, but if my hunch is right, ZP has fresh horses waiting for them west of here. He won't stop. He knows how to put distance between himself and a posse."

"Well, we'll see about that," Keller said.

Joby reined up at the house and dismounted.

"Water your horses, Tom. I'll just talk to the boys some and get my gear, strap on my hogleg and fetch my Henry."

"Don't be too long, Joby. Time's a-wastin'."

Joby wrapped his reins around the hitchrail and walked over to his sons, who still stood there, mouths wide open, bandannas puddled around their necks like red wattles on a turkey.

Keller and the posse dismounted and the men began to stretch their legs. Dolores tied her horse to the hitchrail and walked over to the porch, her dulcimer and case still slung over her shoulder, and stood in the shade, as if unwilling to go inside the house where she was raped. The porch faced east, so there was a parallelogram of shade that the overhanging roof created. Dolores became part of the shadow, and Joby thought she shuddered as if from a sudden and inexplicable chill.

Joby walked over to his sons and extended his arms, touching each on a shoulder.

"Pa, why are all these men here?" Forrest asked.

"A posse. There were some killings in Gilmet. And, the killers robbed the bank there."

"Holy smoke," Mark said, then left his mouth open again to gape at the men walking around.

Forrest suppressed a titter. "Well, there's smoke all right. Pa, we burnt them horses. Poured coal oil all over 'em and set 'em afire."

"I know. You boys did a good job."

"What's Auntie Dolores doin' here?" Mark asked, finally coming to his senses.

"Long story. Boys, you have to stay here, look after the place. I probably won't be gone long."

"But you said you were takin' us with you," Mark protested.

"That's right," Forrest said. "We done packed some of that jerky and hardtack Ma kept by for our hunting trips and we got some airtights with peaches and apricots and some dried persimmons . . ."

"Boys, your grandma is dead. Those bastards murdered her." Joby said it and then pulled his boys close to him in a double embrace. "Aunt Do and I just buried her a while ago. Next to your grandpa."

"Huh?" Mark uttered.

"No," Forrest said.

And in the silence that Joby left to them, they broke down and began to cry. Their bodies shook against his legs and chest and he squeezed them even tighter. He could feel their grief seep through to him, once again, and he fought back the tears that welled up, unbidden, in his eyes. Their sobs tore at him like the lashes of a quirt and he knew he had just destroyed another part of their already shattered world. He knew how much they loved his mother, how much tenderness and caring she had shown them over the years, and he knew they would always have a big hole in their lives where their grandmother once had dwelled. It was a terrible moment for the three of them and Joby knew their hearts were broken, and that his was broken, too, and the pain was squeezing what was leftover.

"Oh, Pa," Mark sobbed. "Not Grandma."

"I'm sorry, Mark. I know you boys loved her."

"We love her still," Forrest said, his voice drenched and sodden with his sobs.

"That's why I've got to leave right away with that posse.

And it would be best if you two stayed here and kept an eye on the place."

Mark broke free of his father's arm first. Then, Forrest stepped aside. They both looked at their father and the expression on their faces was a mixture of sadness and rage.

"You can't leave us here, Pa," Forrest said. "You promised."

"Yeah, you promised," Mark agreed.

"It's just too dangerous. I don't want anything to happen to you two. I've lost my mother, your grandma, and they have your mother. These are very bad men."

"We're not afraid," Forrest said.

Then Mark's expression changed. He blinked his dark eyes in the glare of the sun and looked back at the porch, at that place where Dolores stood in the flap of shade in front of the porch.

"Are you takin' Auntie Do with you, Pa?" Mark asked.

Joby sucked in a breath, as if he was burying a lie that he was about to tell his sons.

"You are, aren't you?" Forrest said. "You're takin' Auntie Do with you and she ain't no older'n Mark and I'm older'n she is."

"You'd take your sister and leave us behind?" Mark asked, his accusatory tone stabbing at Joby like a surgeon's lancet. "That ain't fair, Pa."

"I'm just trying to cut my losses," Joby said, and was immediately sorry that he had said it. He was being unfair, but his heart was sick over his mother's death, his sister's rape and the kidnapping of his wife. He was thinking of how much he had lost, how much he might lose if he took his boys on this dangerous hunt for a pack of murderers.

"Pa, we made packs for the spare horses," Forrest said. "We filled them with grain, cracked corn and wheat. We packed coffee, sugar, pots, pans, plates, cups and everything we need."

"And all the stock has plenty of graze and water, if we're gone a long time," Mark said. "Grandma doesn't have no stock, so there's nothing to look after over at her place."

"You boys make some good arguing," Joby said.

"Then take us with you," Forrest said. "We can take care of the horses and help with a lot of stuff. We've got guns and plenty of cartridges. And I got into that tin Ma keeps hidden in the cupboard and took out all the cash in case you might need it."

Joby was impressed. He sighed and looked at his boys, looked into their eyes, looked at the eager, questioning expressions on their young faces. They were good boys, and their mother had been taken from them. They had a big stake in the hunt for the outlaws, too. As big as his stake, when you came right down to it. He was weakening, and they weren't helping any. In their eyes, he saw a pleading that wrenched at his heart, a fire that might have come from his own eyes at one time, as when he went off to war with the Second Texas and just before that first battle, and all the battles that followed.

"Yeah, you both argue real good," Joby said. "I'm thinking you could be useful."

"Oh, yes," the boys chorused.

"Real useful, Pa," Forrest said, a grin beginning to break on his face, as if he knew the outcome of their conversation. As if he knew that he and Mark had won this particular debate.

"I tell you what," Joby said. "I'll take you along on one condition."

"What's that?" Forrest asked. Mark seemed to lean forward as if he had wanted to ask the same question, but Forrest had beaten him to it.

"You stay out of the way of that posse when we're riding. Ride drag, eat the dust. If you complain just once, or if you cause any ruckus or trouble, I send you back, both of you. Clear?"

Both boys nodded with almost excessive eagerness.

"We will," Mark said. "Do what you say, I mean."

"I know you will," Joby said. "Did you pack bedrolls for all of us?"

"We sure did," Forrest said. "We thought of everything. Matches, paper to start a fire, a hatchet, and we got our knives. Lots of bullets."

Joby grinned.

"And you mind your Aunt Dolores, too," he said. "You can help her cook and clean up our camps."

"Oh, we sure will," Mark said.

"Uh-huh," Forrest agreed.

"All right. Fetch the horses we're taking, lock the house. Did you boys eat anything?"

"We're not hungry," Forrest said.

"Not hungry," Mark said.

"You will be," Joby said. "And you'll be stiff and sore tonight and worse tomorrow and worse the day after. This isn't a camping trip to the back pasture. It's going to be a long, hard ride."

"We can't wait to see Ma," Forrest said.

"And bring her back," Mark added.

Joby nodded and walked back to the house to talk to his sister. The boys started running toward the barn, passing the sundial in the front yard. Joby paused there and saw the shadow edging toward the Roman numeral II and felt his stomach swirl with hunger.

But there was no time to stop and eat. The day was getting short and ZP and his cronies were getting farther and farther away with every passing moment.

"You're taking the boys, aren't you?" Dolores said to him, her face in shadow beneath the porch roof. "I knew you would."

"You look after them, Do. They'll help you cook and clean up at camp."

"I'm glad they're coming," she said.

"You three will ride drag. Out of the way. Understood?"

"You're still as bossy as you were when we were growing up, Joby."

"You're still growing up, sugar."

She smiled wanly and touched Joby's arm.

"Today, I feel real old," she said.

And Joby knew what she meant. He thought of their mother in the ground, lost to them for the rest of their lives. It was all so sad.

"Life," he said. "It's a wonderful thing when it's going along real smooth. But it isn't smooth all the time. Living is what we do when bad things happen."

"And what we think we can never do again," she said. "Go on living. But Ma did that when Pa died. And we'll do it now that she's gone. Right?"

Joby nodded. The posse was remounting as the boys led the horses out of the barn. It was time to go. They'd have to keep their feelings to themselves for now. Life had caught up to them, and had delivered them a new set of rules and a blank map they had to follow.

Maybe that was what life was, he thought. A blank map that you had to chart as you went along. And once you learned all the secrets, you didn't need them anymore. Because that was when you died.

17

SHERIFF TOM KELLER WAS ALREADY COUNTING HIS CHICKENS before they hatched. Joby, Roland and Millpas were ranging far ahead of the rest of the posse, and the tracking seemed almost too easy. Even he and Bill McKinney could follow the trail the outlaws had taken. ZP and his bunch had not tried to cover their tracks. They were staying to the rutted road that led westward from Redmond's place, and although they weren't dawdling, they weren't wearing out leather, either.

An hour after leaving the Redmond place, the sun sailed across the clear, blue sky on its descending arc, turning the earth into an airless furnace. The riders began to believe they were floating in a blazing cauldron as sweat dripped from their brows and stung their eyes. Their clothes were soaked and they began to smell as rank as their horses. The horses were sleek and shiny with sweat, their tails switching at stinging flies, their hides rippling with their twitching muscles, their rubbery nostrils drying out, their mouths slack and open, dripping foamy saliva that caked with dust.

The dust made the riders owl-eyed as it caked the sweat,

forming rings of dirt above their cheeks, and all the shade was caught in the piney woods, without a trace of it on the barren, hoof-scarred road.

"Damn, it's sure hot," Gordon Keith said, wiping his face with his bandanna, which was already soaked through.

"Hotter'n a two-dollar pistol on sale for two bits," Bill Theodore said, splashing water from his canteen into his hat and down the front of his shirt.

"You should have brought yourself a parasol," Robert Myers cracked, sitting tall in the saddle, sweat stains under his armpits and shirt plastered to his back. But his bandanna was damp from canteen water and served to keep him cooler than some of the others.

"I hope we catch those jaspers today," Norman Lozier said. "I don't think I could take another day of this heat."

Keller made no comment. Men always griped about the heat, and this was not serious. Yet. But he had no illusions about catching up to ZP and his gang on that day. He would be happy if they just gained an hour or two on them.

"It is damned hot," McKinney said, almost in a whisper, as he rode alongside the sheriff.

"It's just as hot for them as it is for us, Bill."

"This is the kind of heat that sucks all the sap out of a man."

"You can always go back home and sit in the shade and sip lemonade," Keller said.

McKinney stiffened.

"I'm not going home until I have my daughter with me. Poor girl, I know she must be suffering in this boiling sun as much as I am."

"Bill, you talk too damned much. Save your breath. It'll seem a lot cooler without you flappin' your mouth."

"Talkin' helps pass the time, Tom."

"Well, pass the time somewhere else, then. My mind is on other things. I don't need you actin' like a damned thermometer. I know it's hot and so does everybody else out in this infernal sun."

"I got somethin' else on my mind, too, Tom."

"Well, spit it out, long as it don't have nothin' to do with the sun or the damned heat."

McKinney dabbed at the sweat oiling his neck. He used a white handkerchief from his pocket. He had no bandanna. He blinked his eyes, which were stinging from the dripping sweat.

"This Joby Redmond. And his family. What do you know about him, anyways?"

"His folks came out from Kentucky," Keller said. "His pa was a hard worker, got him some land and died from wounds he got fightin' the damned Apaches. Joby's ma was a plain, homespun woman, who set a fine table, lost her a baby in childbirth in between havin' Joby and his sister, Dolores."

"What about this Joby? I don't know him that well. Seen him in town a time or two, that's all."

"He was in the war. Fought as a Texan in the Second Texas. I know he fought in a lot of big battles, a lot of skirmishes. He ended up a major or a colonel, I forget which. I know that after the war, he got some kind of decoration. For bravery, it was. I know because General Earl Van Dorn hisself come out to Gilmet and pinned the medal on Joby's chest."

"So, Redmond was a hero."

"I know he fought at Shiloh, and was in both battles at Corinth. He never talked about any of it to me nor anybody else."

"He had something to do with this ZP Popper and the other killers?"

"Said he did. They were deserters. Deserted at the second battle of Corinth. Raised a lot of Cain and Joby tracked 'em down, put 'em all in Huntsville. What are you getting at, Bill? Where's all this talk leadin'?"

"Oh, nowheres, I reckon. I was just thinkin' that those killers had help inside the bank and maybe they had help outside, too."

"What in hell are you gettin' at, Bill?"

"Well, we found that ZP's camp and all. And it was right next to where Joby Redmond's folks lived. I just wonder if him and his family was puttin' up those outlaws. Maybe Joby and his family aim to meet up with them later on and split the money."

"Are you plumb crazy, McKinney? Hell, they killed Joby's ma and kidnapped his wife."

"I didn't see no body in that casket, Tom. And maybe Joby wanted us to think his wife was kidnapped."

Keller wheezed through the rising dust and shook his head in disbelief. He looked at McKinney as if to determine if the man was serious or had a bad case of heatstroke.

"Well," Keller said, "you got a lot in your craw, Bill."

"It's all mighty suspicious, Tom. Just too damned many coincidences, if you ask me."

"I'd have to chaw on all that a while, but I think you're a-talkin' through a cocked hat."

"You've got to admit that we've all been bamboozled a mite today. I don't know this Joby Redmond, hardly at all, and maybe his mother ain't dead, and maybe he sent his wife off with that ZP and them just to have her waitin' for him when the rest of us give up."

"You thinkin' about giving up, Bill?"

"Me. No. Not at all. I'd just keep a close eye on Redmond, was I you."

Keller shook his head again, but this time it was as if he was trying to clear it because maybe some of what McKinney was saying made sense. A kind of crazy sense, with all that had happened that day.

And it was true. They hadn't actually seen Joby's

mother in that wooden casket. And he had his whole family with him, his sister and his two boys. It could be that Joby was in cahoots with ZP and that bunch, but it seemed far-fetched.

Nobody in town knew much about Joby Redmond. He kept to himself, bought what he needed when he did come in to Gilmet, didn't engage in small talk. He was polite, and he went to church on Sundays with his mother, sister, wife and sons, but he was known as a taciturn man who did not linger afterward to speak with the members of the congregation. He wasn't unfriendly, Tom knew, he just wasn't overly friendly. People who saw him knew he was some kind of war hero, and they kept their distance, either out of respect or because he did not welcome the handshakers and the backslappers.

But his silence didn't make him a schemer, either, Keller reasoned. And, if Redmond was somehow involved in the bank robbery, the kidnapping and the killings, then that was a pretty big scheme, and it was well covered up.

McKinney spoke no more, and Keller was relieved. He needed to keep his mind on catching ZP and his gang, not worrying about whether or not Joby Redmond and his family were involved. Until he found out different, he believed Joby's mother had been killed and had been in that pine box back there at the old Redmond place.

But still, the doubts lingered, and as the day wore on and the heat worsened, Keller's temper bore a short fuse and he knew he couldn't show that anything was wrong or the whole posse would get infected with his own dark mood.

He looked back once, to see Dolores and her two nephews. They were all riding in the rear of the column, and they seemed as normal as anyone who was eating dust and boiling in the sun. They didn't look like kids who were carrying terrible secrets.

But then, they were cut out of the same cloth as Joby Redmond.

And Joby was something of a mystery.

Deep down, he didn't want to believe that Joby had anything to do with the killings, the robbery or the kidnapping. But there was a connection there. Joby knew ZP, and all the others, and that bunch had used deception when they rode into town and robbed the bank.

ZP had help from inside, from someone who was trusted.

Maybe, as McKinney suspected, ZP was still getting help. From Joby Redmond.

Keller vowed to keep an eye on Joby, to watch him more closely. If he thought Redmond was leading them on a fool's path, he would sure as hell shorten up on the rope.

"Bothers you, don't it?" McKinney said suddenly.

"What?" Keller said.

"That there's more here than meets the eye."

"Bill, you've already worn my ear plumb off. You keep what you told me to yourself and let it go. I'll keep an open mind."

"Fair enough, Tom. That's all I ask."

Keller looked over at McKinney, who seemed to have brightened some, and he was sure that Bill was wearing a smirk on his face.

Then the silence was shattered by someone riding behind Keller. Someone was yelling in a hoarse voice and when he looked back, he saw that it was Billy Brand. Billy was standing up in the stirrups and pointing ahead, pointing to a place high above the tall pines, toward the pale blue sky and the blazing sun.

18

THE COLUMN OF SMOKE ROSE ALMOST LAZILY INTO THE SKY above the trees, white smoke, which soon became mixed with small puffs of ominous black smoke. In the airless heat, the smoke spread only gradually, until it began to hang in a pall over the green tops of the tall pines.

Everyone in the column was talking now, and pointing and commenting.

"Shut up," Keller commanded.

"That's a pretty big fire up there," Uberstrasse said. "And it's not all wood that's burning."

"I know that, Tommy," Keller said.

"I don't like it none," Lozier said, riding up. "That's a house that's burning. I ought to know."

Keller nodded. Norm had lost his home three years before when he was burning leaves and sparks got into his woodshed. The whole town had turned out to fight the fire, but they had all stood around, finally, and watched it burn to the ground. The Lozier family lost everything they owned. It was a sickening sight.

"We'll find out what's going on soon enough," Gordon

Keith said. "Here comes Johnny Roland, riding hell for leather."

Keller wheeled his horse around to see Roland coming toward them at a gallop, whipping and spurring his horse as if somebody were chasing him.

Roland reined up slightly, then turned his horse almost immediately. He panted out a breathless message.

"Come quick. House on fire. Need help."

He kicked his horse into a gallop and rode away before Keller and the others could react. Then it dawned on the sheriff that someone was in trouble.

"Come on, let's go," Keller shouted, slapping his reins across his horse's rump and digging roweled spurs into the animal's flanks.

The posse came to life and, raising a cloud of dust, all chased after Keller and McKinney. And each of them looked up at the sky and saw the smoke still rising in the air, still spreading out like an enormous shroud.

The road took a bend and Keller saw Roland disappear up ahead, turning onto another road that led through thinned pines. Beyond, he saw a structure blazing through the tall trees. He tried to think of who lived out this far, but could come up with no name that he knew.

As soon as Keller turned into the side road, his blood froze.

That was when he heard the screaming.

A woman was screaming, and there was another one he heard, smaller, somehow, weaker, thinner.

A child.

A child and a woman were both screaming.

19

When Joby and Roland followed the outlaw tracks down the side road leading off the main one, they became wary, uneasy.

"What do you make of it, Joby?"

"They could be getting fresh horses here."

"Or maybe taking another route, heading north?"

"I don't know. Anybody live back in here?"

Roland shrugged.

"Let's get off this road and make a wide circle," Joby said. "They could be waiting in the woods for us."

"Good idea," Roland said, turning his horse. He rode off through the thin patch of pines. There were stumps everywhere, showing him that this particular grove had been timbered off, but the loggers had left enough trees to assure future growth.

Joby angled his horse to the left and, while keeping his eyes on the woods where the road cut through, he entered another part of the forest. Shortly afterward, he caught a glimpse of some man-made structures, a barn, perhaps, some kind of outbuilding, and later, what looked to be a house.

It was very quiet and Joby began to think that ZP had come here, then moved on. But he had not taken the same road out that he had taken in, which could mean that he was familiar with this place. Possibly, he had kept remounts here to help him in his escape after robbing the bank in Gilmet. Joby had never been here before.

Joby emerged from the woods on the other side, but stayed just on the fringe in case someone was trying to get a bead on him. He wasn't expecting an ambush this soon in the hunt, but he knew ZP was canny and capable of springing every kind of surprise.

As he rode closer, Joby saw the house, a barn, a couple of small outbuildings. There was no sign of life. There was some fencing beyond the house and more woods. He saw a large pond, partially sheltered by shade trees, shimmering in the sun like a tilting mirror.

He rode to the road that led into the place and saw Roland approaching from the other side.

"See anything, Joby?"

Joby shook his head.

"It's awful quiet."

"That's what worries me. People live here. The land has been tended. I don't see any stock."

"Nor any folks, neither," Roland said. "It's mighty spooky, you ask me."

Joby nodded. Something was wrong here. There should have been people around. Or signs of people. The house was framed of wood—pine, probably—freshly painted within the last two or three years. The barn and the outbuildings were not painted, but the wood in them looked fresher than the wood on the house. He kept looking, thinking.

"Hello, the house," Joby called, loud enough for anyone inside to hear. Loud enough for anyone in the barn or in the other buildings to hear.

The silence, once his voice faded away, was eerie. He felt as if he had ridden onto a place that was newly deserted, as if anyone who had lived there had just vanished. Without at trace.

"You lag behind me, Johnny," Joby said. "I'm going to ride up for a look-see."

"I'll cover your back, Joby."

Joby slipped his Henry Yellow Boy from its sheath and lay it across the pommel. He had already levered a cartridge into the chamber and left the hammer on half-cock. He kept a thumb on the hammer and started riding toward the house, careful to go at an angle so that he had turning and zigzag room in case someone inside decided to take a potshot at him.

As Joby rode closer to the house, he heard a small, annoying sound, like a cupboard door, or a shutter, banging. The sound was coming from the side of the house, so he edged that way, to his left. He saw a small porch and stairs, and a side door that appeared to be partially open. As he drew still closer, he saw that the door was moving. Not very fast, nor at regular intervals, but definitely moving, banging against the jamb or the baseboard.

Joby lifted the Henry from the pommel and held it next to his right thigh, level with the door. His finger slipped inside the trigger guard and he placed his thumb on the hammer, ready to pull back and fire if he was attacked.

"Hello, the house," Joby called again, in a tentative voice. Not too loud, not too soft. Just enough volume to carry to the doorway. "Anybody home?"

The door banged twice in quick succession and Joby eased the hammer back on his rifle.

"Anybody there?" he called out again.

The door banged three times as if someone was kicking it from the inside.

"Can you hear me?" Joby asked, walking his horse slowly up to the porch.

He heard muffled sounds from the other side of the door.

"If you can't talk, then kick the door again. Real hard."

There was a momentary pause and then the door slammed shut very quickly with a loud rap.

"Are you tied up?" Joby asked. "Kick the door again if this is so."

There was a loud kick at the door and Joby dismounted. He wrapped his reins around one of the railings on the small porch and walked up the steps.

"I'm coming in," he said. "And I'm armed. Step back away from the door, if you can."

Joby waited. He heard muffled sounds and something that sounded like shoes shuffling on a hardwood floor. He pushed the door open slightly with the barrel of the Henry rifle. It was dark inside, but he saw something in a doorway beyond what he took to be a kitchen. Shadows and light, a flickering orange light that was very puzzling.

"I'm coming in," Joby said. "Just hold quiet."

Joby pushed the door open further and then it struck something solid. His stomach fluttered with apprehension, but he stepped inside quickly and took two steps beyond the open door and whirled to his right, swinging the rifle barrel around to bear on whatever was keeping the door from opening all the way.

Lying on the floor was a man, bound and gagged, struggling with his bonds. He had a dish towel stuffed in his mouth and tied in back of his head. His hands and feet were trussed with a lariat, and there were knots and more knots. The man's face was red with exertion, his eyes wide and filled with a glaze of panic, or fear.

Joby reached down and turned the man's head, then deftly unknotted the dish towel. The man spit out the gag and sucked in deep lungfuls of air as if he'd been starving for oxygen.

Then the man held up his hands, or tried to, indicating he would like to be freed of the lariat.

"Cut me loose," the man gasped, his voice a rasp as if his throat had been scraped with a rat-tail file.

Joby drew his knife and knelt down. He lay his rifle flat on the floor and began to cut the rope in several strategic places below the knots. He did the feet first, then the hands until the floor was littered with knotted sections of the lariat. The man rubbed his wrists and tried to get up. But his legs did not serve him well and he kept falling back and teetering.

Joby stood, picking up his rifle as he did so.

"Help me," the man rasped.

Joby extended a hand and the man took it. Joby pulled and leaned backward. The man gained his footing and stood there, weaving slightly, gasping for breath. Then he looked at the doorway to the kitchen, the one Joby had seen through the open door.

That's when Joby smelled coal oil and saw the flicker of light on the doorjamb. It took him several seconds to connect what he was seeing and smelling, the smoke from a wax candle and the reek of flammable coal oil.

He glanced around the room and saw the open cupboards and tins on the counter. There was spilled flour, coffee beans, salt, and sugar all over the floor and countertop, as if the place had been ransacked in a hurry.

"Get out," Joby said, pushing the man toward the side door where he had entered the kitchen.

"No," the man protested, and then they both heard a whooshing sound as if black powder had caught fire.

Joby saw the doorway light up with flames and he heard

more whooshing sounds and then the crackle of burning wood. A river of fire shot through the doorway and streamed toward them, toward the place where the man had been lying, all tied up like an animal in a net.

Joby grabbed the man and shoved him through the door. Then he slammed the door shut, hard. In an instant, inside, he had seen what was happening, and knew enough to keep air away from those flames that were racing into the kitchen, and probably into the rooms beyond, as well. He had seen fire before, knew what a destructive force it was.

The man was bent, doubled-over the porch railing, the wind knocked from his lungs. Joby grabbed him by the back of his collar and dragged him down the steps and away from the house.

Then he let out a holler for Roland. "Come, quick," he said, gesturing toward the other rider waiting at the fringe of the woods. He saw Roland put his horse into a gallop and then ran back over to the porch, grabbed up his reins and led his own horse away from the house. He could see flames flickering in the kitchen window, just beyond the porch. That fire was feeding on dry wood and a lot of other stuff inside the house.

"My sons," the man gasped.

"What?" Joby asked, as he came near the man, whose face was drained of color and whose eyes were wide and shot through with what Joby recognized as fear.

"My—my sons are tied up, like me. Up—upstairs."

"Good lord, man. Is there another way into the house?"

"Front door. Quickest."

"You stay here," Joby commanded, handing the man the reins to his horse. "I'll try to get them out."

"Oh, good God, please," the man pleaded.

Joby raced around the side of the house and clambered up the steps of the front porch, his heart pounding so loud he could hear it throbbing in his temples.

The door was locked. He pushed against it and saw that it gave a little. Joby stepped back and kicked it in. He started to go inside. Then he felt a rush of heated air gush from the open doorway, as if from a blast furnace. The next moment, a huge tongue of flame lashed out through the door and Joby jumped back just before it would have struck him.

"Joby, get away," yelled Roland.

Just before Joby turned to leave the porch, the entire door burst into flames and the glass in the front windows exploded, sending showers of sparks and glass spewing from the front room.

The man, leading Joby's horse, came running around the side of the house, yelling hoarsely.

"Save my boys, please save my boys."

Roland reined up and looked at the house. The lower part was engulfed in flames.

"What the hell . . . ?"

"That man's sons are tied up," Joby said, "upstairs. I've got to get them out."

"Man, you can't go in there. You'll be burned alive."

Joby turned to the man he had rescued.

"Have you got a long ladder that will reach up to the second story of your house?"

The man nodded.

"In the barn," he said, pointing to the barn. "But, I think . . ."

He never finished his sentence. As all three men watched, the barn caught fire, and in seconds was engulfed in raging flames.

"Johnny, go get the others. Quick. We need help here. Bad."

Roland turned his horse and lit out at a gallop.

"It'll be too late," the man said. "They poured coal oil all through the house, upstairs and down."

Joby knew who the man was talking about.

"My wife—she's up there, too," the man said. "In our bedroom. Oh, God."

Joby's heart sank like a stone in a murky well, down into a darkness that was deeper than the darkest night. He looked again at the barn, and knew it was hopeless to go there. He looked at the lariat on his own horse. He wondered if he could tie something to the end of it and throw it through an upstairs window, hoping it would catch enough so that it would hold him while he climbed up and got the woman and those boys out before it was too late.

"Have you got a chunk of metal, like a moldboard plow or something I could tie to my rope?" Joby asked. "Something out in the open? Where we can get to it?"

The man hesitated, as if thinking, and then they heard the other windows in the bottom part of the house explode and the flames ate at the wood with a fierce hunger, devouring the siding even as it turned black from the scorching tendrils of fire.

Johnny went for his rope, listening for an answer that seemed as if it would never come.

20

PRECIOUS SECONDS WERE TICKING BY AND JOBY KNEW HE HAD to act fast or more lives would be lost.

"Snap out of it, man," he said. "I need a chunk of metal to sling up there through a window so I can climb up and get your folks out of that second story."

The man stared at the burning house as if he were in a hypnotic trance. Joby slapped him on the cheek, then grabbed his shoulder and shook him.

"What's your name?" Joby asked, hoping to bring the man back to reality.

"Sam. Sam Cherry."

"Sam, I need a plow, or a chunk of angle iron . . . anything heavy enough to hold back of a window."

"There's an old plow out by the barn."

"Get it. Run as fast as you can, Sam, and get that plow and bring it to me."

Joby slammed the Henry back in its sheath and untied the dally thongs holding his lariat to his saddle. He shook out the rope and held one end while he measured, with his eye, the distance he'd have to sling a weight up to the second story of the burning house.

The fire began to generate a wind that swirled around and above the house, and Joby knew it would not be long before the entire structure was engulfed in flames. The porch roof sloped away from the second story and there was little footing on it. Still, he figured that if he could get a rope secured in the middle window, he could climb up it and untie the people inside. If Keller and the posse arrived in time, they would have enough manpower to catch those he got out through the window.

Joby looked toward the barn. He saw Sam bend over and pick up something, then run back with it. The man was covered in sparks from the burning barn, which winked in his hair like fireflies, but these blew out as he ran toward Joby.

Joby beckoned to Sam, urging him to hurry. He tried to see what it was he was carrying. It was not part of a plow, but something smaller.

"This is all I could find," Sam said, panting from the exertion. He held up a broken pitchfork. The fork was rusted, but it had four strong tines. The handle was broken off, but what remained was still attached to the fork. He thrust it at Joby.

"This will do fine, I think," Joby said.

Quickly, Joby tied the rope onto the base of the fork, looping the lariat over the base and around two of the tines, then onto the handle, weaving line over the others, crisscrossing them. Then he tied a strong knot, and another for good measure.

"This ought to do it," Joby said, as he approached the house, holding the pitchfork up and trailing the rope behind him. He began to swing the pitchfork as if he were going to rope a calf. Faster and faster the rope twirled over his head until Joby released the pitchfork. The tool arced high in the air and struck the wall next to the window, then slid back down over the roof.

"You were close," Sam said.

"I'll get it this time."

Joby started swinging the rope again, and when it was going very fast, he lunged, opening his hand so that the fork flew out and made less of an arc as it streaked toward the window.

There was a crashing of glass as the pitchfork broke through the window, smashing into the top floor. Joby slowly pulled on the rope until he felt the fork jam up against the inside wall.

"Now," he said, "I hope it holds. I'm going to climb up there and find your folks, if I can."

"I'll go up after you."

"No, you stay down here. You may have to catch anyone I get out."

"All right," Sam said.

"Help boost me up to the roof," Joby said. He knew he had to get up that high before he could pull himself up the rest of the way.

Joby had already determined that he could probably climb one of the corner posts and get onto the steep roof, but that would take too much time. The flames were raging more fiercely now in the lower part of the house and he could see that they were attacking the ceilings on the first floor.

Sam half-squatted, his feet spread wide to brace himself for Joby's weight. He interlocked his hands together and held them out for Joby's foot.

Joby put some of the rope over his shoulder and steadied himself on Sam's shoulder as he put a foot on his clasped hands.

"When I get up straight, push up," Joby said.

"Will do."

Joby took a quick breath and then mounted Sam's hands. He straightened and grabbed the edge of the roof. Sam grunted and lifted upwards. Joby jumped at the same time and sprawled onto the roof. He threw a leg up and crabbed sideways until all of his body was atop the roof. Then he slid along toward the window, bracing himself as he went so that he would not slide off. He pulled on the rope, hoping it would hold.

Then Joby got to his knees and took in rope as he pulled himself toward the shattered window.

With feet widespread, Joby was able to reach the window. He paused for a second or two to catch his breath and then began kicking out the rest of the glass, affording him an entryway through the window.

Joby pulled on the rope one last time and crawled through the window. Tendrils of smoke were leaking up through the floor. He was in a small bedroom. He dropped the rope and looked around. There was a boy tied up at the foot of the bed.

Joby ran to him and removed his gag, then slashed the ropes binding his ankles and wrists.

"Where's your brother and your mother?" Joby asked.

The boy, who could not have been more than seven or eight years old, stared at him stupidly, as if mute.

"The house is on fire," Joby said. "I need to find your mother and your brother. Can you talk?"

The boy nodded. He was scared, Joby knew. Terrified.

"Go wait by that window," Joby said, pointing to the window through which he had just come. "I'll find your brother and your mother."

"Out there," the boy said, pointing to the open doorway.

Joby nodded and dashed from the room. Smoke was rising quickly through cracks in the floor, but he could still see where he was going. He looked around, saw where the stairs were, and the doors to other rooms. The upper level looked down on a large space on the first floor that appeared to be a wide hallway.

Joby called out as he ran to the first room. "Make some noise so I can find you," he shouted.

He entered the room and saw a woman lying trussed up next to a sewing machine. She held her head up and he could see the gag in her mouth. Her eyes were wide with fear. He knelt down beside her and removed her gag. Then he slashed her ropes as she gasped for breath. There was a lot of smoke in the room, and she began to cough.

"Do you have one more son somewhere? I came in through the window in the top bedroom and freed one of them, a young boy, about seven or eight.

"I—I don't know," she said. "My husband . . ."

"He's outside. Go and wait by the window with your other boy. Don't try to get out. I'll have to help you. Do you understand?"

"Yes, I think so," she said.

Joby helped her to her feet. She was a small, nervous woman with light red hair and blue eyes.

"Just wait by the window," Joby said again. "I'll find your other boy and meet you there."

He helped the woman from the room and pointed to the bedroom he had just left. Then he started roaming the top floor looking for the other boy. He heard a thump from one room. The door was closed and he opened it. The room was filled with smoke and he thought he saw flames streaking up next to the baseboards.

"Anybody here?" Joby yelled.

Another thump.

Joby held his breath and entered the smoke-filled room. Another thump, and he turned and saw a bunk bed against the opposite wall. A boy lay on the lower bunk. He, too, was bound and gagged. Swiftly, Joby went to him and removed the cloth from his mouth, then cut the ropes around his ankles and wrists. This boy was older, about twelve or thirteen, Joby guessed, with sandy hair.

"Mister, don't kill me," the boy said.

"Come with me. I'm going to get you out of here."

The boy got up from the bed and started to walk, but his legs gave way. Joby guessed that his blood circulation had been cut off for some time and he was still weak.

He put an arm around the boy, and pulled him to his feet.

Then there was a loud roar and flames shot up through the flooring next to the baseboards and started to engulf the entire room.

Joby fought through the smoke and flames. Fire roared up the stairs and a wall of flame blocked his way. He ducked his head and waited for the flames to subside.

That's when he heard the woman screaming. And the smaller boy began to wail, as well.

"Help, help," cried the woman.

"I'm coming," Joby yelled, but the flames from the stairs still blocked his way. He looked around him. He had to get past those flames to reach that front bedroom, but they had begun eating away at the floor itself. In seconds, he knew, he and the older boy would be consumed by the flames and he never would reach that front bedroom.

The older boy began to tremble and Joby gave him a squeeze.

"We'll get through this," Joby said.

But the woman's frantic screams drowned out his words and the flames began to climb and rush along the ceiling.

Soon, Joby knew, he and the boy would be caught in a flaming tomb and would never get out alive.

21

Beneath the whoosh and rushing sound of flames, Joby heard galloping hoofbeats coming ever closer, increasing in loudness. That was small comfort to him at that moment as he and the boy faced lashing flames coming from the stairs and fire licking at and streaming across the ceiling right in their very path to safety.

Joby had to make an instant decision or he knew they would perish. Long before they burned, they would die from the smoke that would soon fill their lungs. He turned to the boy, who seemed rooted to the floor, paralyzed in the face of that terrible wall of flames.

"We're going to get through, son," Joby said. "I'm going to carry you. Just relax."

"No," the boy cried, starting to back away.

Joby grabbed him and pulled him back. Then, with a single smooth motion, he bent down and slung the boy over his shoulder.

"Hold your breath," Joby said.

He held up one hand to shield his face, his eyes and nose, then waited until the flames subsided a fraction. The woman and boy in the front bedroom were still screaming, crying out for help, but he could no longer hear the pounding of horses' hooves on the ground outside. Taking in a deep breath and holding it, Joby ducked and dashed through the flames, running as fast as he could. He felt the heat almost instantly. It seemed to wrap around him and envelop him, and he smelled his hair burning, his eyebrows being singed and his arms beginning to bake.

It seemed an eternity before he cleared the wall of fire, but he found himself on the other side with a clear path to the bedroom up front. He kept on running, gulping in a quick breath of air. He hoped the boy over his shoulder was all right and had not breathed in any smoke or flames during his mad dash through the blazing inferno.

Joby flipped the now squirming boy off his shoulder as he entered the bedroom. Flames were slithering up next to the baseboards in there and the woman and her other son were flattened against the wall next to the window, both screaming at the tops of their lungs.

Joby checked the boy he had carried through the flames and saw that he was shaken, but all right. He walked over to the woman and her other son, grabbed her by the shoulders and shook her.

"Stop," he said in a calm voice. "We're going to get you and your boys out of here."

The woman looked at him in terror, as if he were some kind of demon bent on murdering her. He could understand that, after what she had been through. She didn't know him. For all she knew, he might have been one of that bunch who had tied her up and had come back to kill her and her sons.

"See that broken pitchfork there, under the window?" he asked when she stopped screaming. He pointed. She looked down at it and nodded.

"That's how I got up here. There's a rope outside. Can you climb down it?"

She shook her head, that look of terror still flaring in her eyes.

Joby looked back at the boy he had carried into the room.

"You ever do any rope climbing?" Joby asked.

The boy nodded.

"Come here." Joby walked to the window and looked out. The posse was there, some were dismounting, others just stared from their saddles at the burning house. Joby waved and cupped his hands over his mouth.

"We're coming out," he said. "Somebody get at the other end of this rope." He reached down and jiggled the rope. Then he ducked his head back inside.

He turned back to the older boy. "Just take your time," he said. "Grab that rope real tight with both hands and let yourself down to the edge of the roof. Stay on your belly. Then, ease your legs over the roof and climb down to the ground. Can you do that?"

"I-I think so," the boy said. His voice cracked. It was changing, so Joby figured he must be about thirteen years old.

"Do it," Joby said. "I'll help you out the window."

The boy crawled out the window and grabbed the rope with both hands. But he was facing the wrong way.

"Turn around," Joby told him, but don't let loose of the rope. Face me, then drop to your knees and crawl backward. Hold onto that rope real tight."

The boy did as he was told and soon he was crawling backward down the sloping roof. Joby watched, his nerves jangling at how long it was taking. When he saw the boy disappear over the edge of the roof, he turned away from the window.

He walked back to the door and closed it tightly. There

was too much air in the room and he was worried about those flames along the baseboards. Outside the room, the fire was roaring as it raged across the ceiling and floor, devouring the wood and everything in its path.

"Now, lady," Joby said. "I'm going to let this boy go out the same way. Can he follow those same instructions?"

"Y-yes, I think so. Danny, can you climb down the rope?"

The boy was frozen with fear. But he nodded.

Joby helped Danny climb through the window, making sure his hands were gripped tightly around the rope. The boy's hands were trembling and his fingers kept slipping off even before he started backing down over the roof.

"If you can't do this, I can carry you down, Danny," Joby said. "But, you'll have to wait until your mother goes before I can take you with me."

"N-no, I'll do it," Danny said, his lower lip quivering as he began to whimper.

"Are you sure?"

"Pretty sure."

"You've got to be real sure, Danny."

Joby realized that the boy's mother had clasped his sleeve with her hand and was kneading the cloth with her fingers, pulling on the sleeve as if she were drowning.

"I can do it."

"Real slow, then. Get the rope between your feet, too, and clamp those tight against it."

The boy's legs moved as he tried to get the rope between his shoes. Finally, he managed it and then he began to ease down the rope.

"Don't look at your feet, Danny," Joby said. "Just look at me and your mother."

"A-all right."

"He'll fall," his mother said. "He'll break his little neck."

"Just be quiet, ma'am."

Her hands shook as she pulled on his shirt sleeve. Joby reached up and put his hand over her fingers, then rubbed them to soothe her fears.

Joby could hear the fire raging outside the door and the room where he and the woman waited was filling with smoke. He heard crackling sounds inside the room. He turned quickly to look at the baseboards and saw that the flames had increased. The room grew very hot and the smoke intensified. He knew that they could not stay there much longer.

"Faster, Danny," the boy's mother said. "Just a little faster."

The boy was halfway down the roof. He looked tearfully at his mother and tried to smile. But he was scared, Joby knew, and his body was shaking all over now.

"What's your name, ma'am?" Joby asked, to get her mind off of her son and the danger of his falling.

"Livia," she said.

"Pretty name. I'm Joby."

"I can hardly breathe," she said.

"Stick your head out the window, Livia."

"We could be burned alive in here."

"Don't think about that."

Danny reached the edge of the roof. Then he stopped.

"Go on," Joby said. "Just push out slowly and let your legs fall over the edge of the roof."

"I-I'm scared," he said.

"Someone will catch you if you fall," Joby said.

He looked down at the people watching the boy. Keller and McKinney were still on horseback, and so were his sons and Dolores. He could see three or four others, while some were out of view, probably watching for the boy to come the rest of the way down the rope.

McKinney, Joby noticed, was holding a hand over his

mouth and coughing. He was bent over his saddle and seemed to be struggling for his breath. Joby wondered if the smoke had gotten into McKinney's lungs or if he was just overcome with emotion. What with all the screams and the fire, Joby couldn't blame him much.

"Danny, push off the roof, but hold tight to that rope," Joby said, seeing that the boy was still afraid to go over the edge. Into the unknown. He'd had similar feelings when he was that age. Like the first time he went to the swimming hole with the older boys. He had never swum before and, at first, he was terrified of the water. The older boys had goaded him and taunted him, but he balked, because when he looked down at the water, so dark and deep, he saw death waiting for him. He saw his lungs filling up with water and his body sinking to the bottom like a stone.

One boy had made the others shut up and he had talked to Joby, explaining that no one there would let him drown. He told Joby to hold his breath and close his eyes and just jump in. He told Joby to push his hands against the water and he would rise to the surface. Then he could open his eyes and laugh.

"You can laugh at death, because you beat it, Joby," the boy had said. "And, you will learn to swim like the rest of us, and that water will seem like another home to you."

Finally, Joby remembered, he had jumped in and done what the older boy had told him to do. He was scared out of his wits when he sank down, but he paddled his hands and kicked his feet, like a frog, and he had come up into the sunlight and the boys had all cheered him and he gulped in air and realized that he had not drowned, that he was alive and that he had overcome a big fear.

"Go on, Danny," Joby said, in a soothing tone. "You're a big boy, like your brother. It will only last a minute and then you'll be on your way down that rope."

"Please, Danny," his mother pleaded. "We have to get out of this burning house or we'll die."

Danny's face changed, then. Joby could see that the boy was thinking. Thinking hard. And the boy was making a decision. A decision to push off that roof and climb down the rope to safety.

Joby said nothing. He wanted Danny to make the decision on his own, to feel the triumph of victory when he overcame his fears and left the seeming safety of the roof.

And then the decision was made for Danny. It was made for Joby and Livia, as well.

Joby heard the crackling of the fire, louder now than before, and then he felt and heard a rush of heat, like the air from a blast furnace. He turned and saw the door to the bedroom blow inward, its wood encased in a shroud of flames. Behind it, from outside the room, a wall of flame rushed into the opening like water through a funnel. In a fraction of a second, the entire room seemed to burst into flames and there was no longer any air to breathe. There was only that smashing ball of flame and the searing heat that probed at their bodies, draining them of moisture, sucking away the last of their breath, and lashing flames that seemed to possess a thousand fingers, each one stretching out for them like the very hands of death.

22

SHERIFF KELLER WAS THE FIRST TO SEE THE DANGER FROM the ground. He shouted, "Look out," and the others looked up and saw the top of the house and gasped.

Danny pushed off the roof and lost his grip on the rope. He fell, a scream ripping from his throat and issuing from his mouth, piercing, high-pitched, curdled with terror.

Joby felt the explosive force of the flames and pushed Livia through the window. Then he felt himself being hurled right after her, as if the room had exploded. He heard the sound of glass shattering and felt the sting of glass splinters knifing into his neck and back. He grabbed Livia around the waist and she twisted as if to get away, but Joby realized that they were falling, sliding down the sloping roof. He dug his bootheels into the shingles trying to stop their downward progress, and felt the roof grate against them. He and Livia tumbled then steadied into a sickening slide. He saw Livia's hand shoot out, as she tried to grab the rope that lay like a snake across the roof.

Joby reached for the rope, too, knowing it was useless at that point. His hand touched it and he felt the burn of it across his palm and then, they both struck the edge of the roof, seemed to hang there for one short eternal moment, and then his stomach stayed up in the air as his body plummeted downward. Livia slipped from his grasp and he knew she would hit the ground first.

Joby saw, just before he struck the ground, that the boy, Danny, was out of the way, and that Livia had been caught by two men he could not immediately recognize. He saw them stagger backward under her weight and then he hit the ground himself. But he was surprised that he did not wind up with a mouthful of dirt and that the landing was softer than he had expected.

As soon as the stars stopped dancing in his head, Joby felt hands on his body and the next thing he knew he was being dragged away from the house. He looked back at the place where he had landed and saw a pile of slickers stacked there. Not as soft as a mattress, he thought, but a hell of a lot softer than the bare ground.

"He's breathin'," someone said.

"I don't think none of his bones is broke," another said.

Joby's brain was still filled with fuzz, so he could not determine those who had spoken, but he began to feel better almost immediately. And with the heat from the burning house diminishing, his head began to clear.

"I'm all right," Joby said. "I can walk. I think."

"You and that woman what fell off'n the roof gave us quite a scare," one of the men said. Joby looked at him, recognized Billy Brand. The other man who had helped him away from the conflagration was Norm Lozier.

"Well, I think I scared hell out of myself," Joby said, a wry grin playing on his lips.

Joby reached down and dusted himself off, then

slapped both men on the upper arms in gratitude. He walked over to where Sam and Livia stood, embracing each other. Danny still sat on the ground, looking dazed. The older boy stared at the burning house, his face a mirror of sadness and fear, and perhaps more than a trace of disbelief.

"Thanks, Mister Redmond, for gettin' my wife and boys out of that house."

Sam broke the embrace and looked at Joby. Livia was crying and seemed so stricken that she could not speak. But she nodded and Joby understood.

"I'm mighty glad you got me out, too," the older boy said, holding out his hand. "I'm Neely."

"I wondered what your name was," Joby said. "Glad you all made it."

"Glad you happened along," Sam said.

"I'm sorry you lost all you had here," Joby said.

"It could have been worse," Sam said. "Lots worse."

Keller dismounted and walked over, glancing briefly at Joby, but then looking Sam square in the eye. Men began picking up their slickers and refolding them as they moved away from the heat of the burning house. Dolores, Mark and Forrest picked up their slickers and started to repack them behind the cantles of their saddles.

"Can you tell me how you got yourself in this fix, Mister?" Keller asked.

"You mean those men?"

"I do. How long ago did they leave and what did they do when they were here?"

"They were gone about an hour or so before you come up."

"How in hell did that fire start?" Keller asked Cherry.

"That man they called ZP got some candles and lit 'em after his men poured coal oil all over the house."

Cherry seemed dazed to the point of idiocy as he continued staring at the conflagration that was consuming his house. His wife, Livia, was also in a state of shock, standing there, her face drained of color beneath the soot that marked her fair complexion with shadowy stains. The two boys were quietly weeping, tears streaming down their faces.

"That's a trick ZP has used before," Joby said. "A way to slow us down. He knows the candles will burn down and ignite the liquid fuel. Creates quite a distraction, and keeps whoever's chasing him busy while he eats up miles getting the hell away."

"He's a bastard," McKinney said.

"Mr. Cherry," Keller said. "What are you going to do?"

Cherry looked away from the house toward the barn and tears filled his eyes. He shook his head in bewilderment. "I—I don't rightly know," he said. He looked at his wife. "Livia?"

She sighed and her mouth tightened into a frown. A look of defiance came into her eyes for a brief moment, and then was replaced with the murky light of dejection as her features sagged in resignation.

"I—I can't face it no more," she said. "I want to get as far away from here as I can, Sam. There—there's just nothing left. Everything we own . . ."

Her sadness seemed infectious and those around her hung their heads in dejected silence. Some of the men examined their boots and began worrying the dirt underfoot with their heels and toes as if trying to rearrange a small part of a universe that had been shattered.

"Maybe we'll go into Gilmet," Cherry said. "Livia's got kin there."

"We'll have to walk it," Livia said. "Before those evil men burned our barn down they shot and killed all our stock, including our horses. Our wagon was in that barn, too. There's just nothing left. Nothing."

Keller's facial features softened as he looked at Livia Cherry. He cleared his throat as if he were on the verge of making a speech at a place where talking was not allowed.

"Ma'am, we can spare some men to ride you and your family back to Gilmet. If that would help."

"I'd be mighty grateful," Livia said to the sheriff, a pleading in her eyes that seemed close to desperation.

Keller looked around him at the men gathered there.

"Maybe your two boys and your sister," Keller offered, looking straight at Joby.

"Not us," Forrest said. Mark nodded in agreement.

"I'm not going back to Gilmet either," Dolores said. Her eyes flashed with the sparks of defiance.

Keller looked around at the others. Some avoided his gaze. One who didn't was Tommy Uberstrasse.

"Tommy?" Keller said.

"I'm ready to go back, Tom. I can't take much more of this. Those robbers are animals. 'Sides, I got chores to do."

"Anybody else?" Keller asked.

"I'll go with Tommy," Billy Brand said, looking at Norm Lozier. "Norm, you want to give this up, take these poor folks back to town?"

Lozier nodded.

Robert Myers held up his hand. "I've got a heap to do back to home, Tom. I'll ride one of these folks back to town."

"That'll be enough, then," Keller said. "We can do without them, Joby, don't you think?"

Joby exhaled through his nostrils. He nodded. He was sore from the fall and had watched the sun crawl across the sky, realizing they had lost valuable time, just as Popper had planned. He would feel better if Keller and the other posse members all went back to Gilmet.

"We can do without most of those you brought with you, Tom."

"You and your sister and your boys can't face all them outlaws by yourselves, Joby."

"Nobody's going to face anybody the longer we stand around here jawin', Tom. Popper's putting miles under him and the day's getting away from us."

"I agree. We'll track until dark and then make camp. Tommy, you do what you have to do here. Norm, Billy. Robert. We're going to ride out and continue our pursuit of those bank robbers."

Uberstrasse nodded, took Livia's arm and began leading her toward his horse. Myers, Lozier and Brand brought their horses up and began talking quietly with Sam Cherry and his two sons.

Keller climbed back on his horse. Joby nodded to Dolores and his sons, then walked to his horse. Johnny Roland, already mounted, was holding the reins for Joby.

"Thanks, Johnny."

"You fit to ride, Joby?"

"I'd ride if I was dead, Johnny. You know that."

"I reckon."

"Let's get on that track. The others can catch up. Millpas, you better come with us. We'll be scouting a place for the night, too, and you can be the messenger when we find a spot."

"I'd rather take back a message that we've done caught them jaspers and put 'em all to sleep."

"Unless they all got crippled real sudden, that's not going to happen," Joby said.

"You have any idea where Popper might be headed?" Roland asked.

Joby shook his head as he clucked to his horse. He waved to Dolores and his sons and kicked his horse into a trot, his eyes scanning the ground for tracks so that he would be accustomed to looking for them when they got back out to the road. He did not look back at Keller and the others, but he heard his name called and turned around.

"Mister Joby, thanks," Livia Cherry called. "We're mighty grateful to you."

Joby lifted a hand in acknowledgment and turned back around, heaving a sigh. It had been a close call for that family. Others, in the past, who had run into Popper and his bunch had not been so lucky.

After he, Millpas and Roland regained the road and picked up Popper's tracks coming out of the woods some distance away from the Cherry place, Joby glanced up at the sun.

He figured they'd be lucky to have three more hours of daylight left. If he were riding alone, he could keep tracking until he could no longer see the ground. But there was the posse, and his sister and his sons. They would be dog-tired by sundown, and hungry.

That was the trouble with a group of people. You had to travel the speed of the slowest one, and you were hampered by the weakest. The posse had thinned out, but not nearly enough to suit Joby.

He wondered how long Keller and the others he had brought with him would last. Another day? Two? He'd bet none of them would have the stomach to last even a week. The further they rode, the further away from home they'd all be, and these were family men and they had other concerns back in civilization. He'd give most of them another day.

The only one he didn't know about was McKinney. He hoped he would tire of the journey, the tracking, the heat, and the bone-jarring ride in the saddle. But he couldn't count on it. McKinney might be the type who would die before he would quit. Or he just might be stubborn enough to go on even after he had been rendered helpless by fatigue and hunger and thirst.

Joby just didn't know. But of all those men he hoped would go back to town, Bill McKinney was at the top of his list.

23

THE TRACKS OF POPPER AND HIS MEN GREW MORE CONFUSING shortly after Joby, Roland and Millpas left the Cherry spread. It took Joby a while to decipher them, and when he went over them again with Milpas and Roland, he realized what Popper had done, and how he had done it.

"He took horses from Sam Cherry," Joby said.

"Looks that way," Roland said.

"But he wanted us to be in the dark about it for a while."

"Someone, two riders, I figure," Millpas said, "joined him here. They came out of the woods leading five horses."

"They'll wear theirs out pretty soon," Joby said. "ZP's got a habit of doing that."

"You know that jasper pretty well, don't you, Redmond?" Millpas said. "Maybe you know all of 'em."

"I know 'em."

"Maybe you used to ride with them." There was an underlying accusation in Millpas's words, and a trace of sarcasm.

"You don't listen well, do you, Millpas?"

"I listen good enough."

"We were all in the Second Texas. ZP and the others deserted. I tracked them down after we finished up at Corinth. So, yeah, I know them pretty well. But not in the way you mean."

"What way do I mean?" There was now a belligerence in Millpas's voice.

"Any way you want what you say to mean."

"Yeah? Well, I put it pretty plain to you, Redmond. I think you was thick with these *hombres* and maybe you're still thick with 'em."

"Ease on back, Bob," Roland said.

"I'll ease up, soon's I get some answers from Redmond here," Millpas said. "He's just too mighty familiar with this ZP and his bunch to suit me. He might be leadin' us all on a wild goose chase. Maybe takin' us up to where they can all jump us and wipe us out."

"You figger that?" Joby said, looking Millpas square in the eyes.

"I'm beginnin' to figger just that, Redmond."

"Well, why don't you just go on back to Gilmet, then? I don't need you to track or help me none."

"I didn't ask to come with Tom, neither," Millpas said. "I just figgered I owed them folks in Gilmet something."

"Well, you don't owe me."

"I ought to throw down on you right here and now, Joby Redmond, and settle all doubts once and for all."

Roland's face darkened as he saw Millpas extend the fingers of his right hand and raise it slightly as if he were going for the pistol holstered on his gunbelt.

"Bob, hold on," Roland said. "They ain't no call for you to make war talk with Redmond, here. He ain't done nothin'."

"How do you know that, Johnny? I'm thinkin' he might have set up that whole thing back there in Gilmet. Told that Popper about the bank and all. Then had Popper take his wife so's to avoid us suspicioning him."

"Millpas," Joby said, "if you touch the butt of that six-shooter, it'll be the last thing you ever do. But before you even think about it, think about this. My sister was raped by that sonofabitch, and he's got my wife and he's probably going to rape her, if he hasn't already. So think about what you've accused me of before you make the next biggest mistake of your life."

Millpas let out a breath and his jaw dropped slightly. Roland stared at Joby, then looked at Millpas. Joby made no move toward his own pistol, but both Gilmet men knew that Joby's drawing hand would not have far to travel.

Millpas dropped his hand.

"I didn't think about your sister, Redmond."

"You didn't think about nothin', Bob," Roland said. "So, make your apologies and let's get on with this. Those tracks are dryin' up in this god-awful heat."

Millpas let his hand drop away from his holster and he drew a deep breath. He looked at Joby and opened his mouth as if to say something. But nothing came out for a long moment. Joby stared him straight in the eyes and, finally, Millpas dropped his head, breaking the gaze between them.

"I—I might have stepped out of line, Redmond," Millpas said, finally. "This whole thing is way out of my quarter section. I need to get back to my own place."

"You're quittin'?" Roland asked Millpas.

Millpas turned his horse in reply.

"That's up to you," Joby said.

"I've had a bellyful of this," Millpas said. "Good luck to you, Johnny, and to both of you'uns. *Adios*."

With that, Millpas jabbed his horse in the flanks with his spurs and headed back down the road, back toward the posse, and perhaps, back to town.

"Bob," Roland called. "Don't quit on us now."

"Johnny, let him go," Joby said. "He's got something

stuck in his craw and nothing I can say is going to wash it down right now."

"Sometimes I think that boy don't have good sense."

"No harm done," Joby said. "Sometimes a man can't help what pops into his mind. Trouble comes when he doesn't know how to get back on the trail and leave that stuff behind."

"I know what you mean, Joby. Me 'n Bob are friends, but I don't know where he got all those crazy ideas."

"I reckon he's not the only one who's wondering about me. If I was in that posse and I run across me in the thick of this, I'd be suspicious, too."

"Well, I ain't. I know you didn't have nothin' to do with all that ruckus in town."

Joby smiled. "Do you, Johnny?"

Roland shot Joby a look and then shook his head.

"Now, don't you go puttin' ideas in my head, Joby Redmond. I don't need 'em."

Joby laughed.

"Let's get to trackin', Johnny. My hunch is that ZP is going to have a few more surprises for us before this hunt is over. And, I do want my wife back before . . ."

Joby didn't finish the sentence, but both men knew what Joby meant. The thought was between them, and it drove them on as they took up the track once again.

They rode into the afternoon of long shadows and Joby knew that ZP did, indeed, have another surprise for them.

"He's sure pushin' them horses of his'n," Johnny said as the sun began to kiss the western horizon.

"He's running them hard," Joby said. "And we're not gaining on him."

"What do you think he's up to?"

"He wants to put some distance between us and he doesn't care that he'll lose a few horses. He has some spares."

"That's right. Them he took from the Cherry place."

"And that is why he took them," Joby said.

"You know him to do this before?"

Joby nodded.

"Popper is a ruthless, desperate man. I think the war set off something inside his skull. Later, I learned that his family had been slaughtered by Comanches out west of here. He was just a kid, but he saw it all. The Comanches raped his mother and his sister right in front of his father and then cut their throats, mutilated them. ZP had to watch it all and then he was taken prisoner. He escaped a couple of years later, but he learned their cruel ways and it must have stuck with him."

Roland swore under his breath.

"Seeing so much when you're young like that can do things to a man."

"But you were in the war. You saw things just as bad."

"Maybe not as bad."

"That don't give him no excuse," Roland said.

"No, there's no excuse for what Popper has done. What he's doing now. I think he's got something all twisted up inside him. Maybe he blames the whole world for what happened to him and his family. I know he blames me for putting him in prison. And he's right. I did put him in prison."

"But he got out."

"Yes, he got out," Joby said. "And I'm wishing now I had put him down when I had the chance."

"You mean shot him in cold blood?"

"Yes. That's what you do when you kill a man. It's always in cold blood. Same as when you shoot a dog with the rabies."

Roland shuddered.

"I don't know if I could do such a thing, Joby."

"Then maybe you ought to join Bob Millpas and ride on back to town."

"What do you mean?"

"Because when I see Popper again, I'm going to kill him. I'm not even going to think twice about it. That man will never face a judge or a jury. Not ever again."

"God."

The two men rode on and neither spoke for a long time. The tree shadows grew longer and the sun began to sink over the horizon before they stopped at a shaded creek that offered shelter for the night. And it was a place, Joby figured, that could be easily defended with a guard or two.

"We'll camp here for the night, Johnny."

"You reckon the posse will find us, or stop somewheres else?"

"Tom Keller knows I'll stop and camp. They'll be along."

Roland shaded his eyes and looked beyond the creek, then turned and looked back up the road.

"They should be along soon," he said.

"Let's start gathering firewood and set up a camp for those folks," Joby said. "Better fill your canteen. I aim to ride out early in the morning."

"Right," Roland said, and jumped down from his horse as if eager to do something so he wouldn't think about what lay ahead of them.

An hour later, Keller and the posse, Joby's sister and his sons rode up. It was already dusk and nearly too dark to see. But Joby had a campfire going and Roland was across the creek, keeping a lookout.

"Figured we'd find you," Keller said. "How much ahead of us is Popper and that bunch?"

"Not far," Joby said. "But they'll put up for the night, same as us."

"Where's Johnny Roland?"

Joby pointed across the creek. The sheriff squinted.

"I see him. What's he doing over yonder?"

"Keeping an eye out. Popper might send a man back down his trail to find out what we're doing."

"Or pick a couple of us off," Keller said.

"That's just exactly what he might do," Joby said, soft enough so that the others could not hear him. "We'll have to set guards for the night."

Keller swung down from his horse.

"What happened between you and Bob Millpas?" Keller asked Joby.

McKinney dismounted and walked over before Joby could answer. He was glowering, and Joby saw that the man seemed to be trying to keep from venting his rage. The veins in his neck stood out like those of a bull in the rut.

"I guess Millpas didn't have the guts for this work," Joby said.

"That's not what he told us," McKinney said.

"Bill, shut up," Keller said.

"I think Redmond here run Millpas off, like he said, because he's in cahoots with Popper and his gang of murderers."

Keller's eyes flared as he shot McKinney a stern look of warning.

"Bill, you'd best keep your thoughts to yourself," Keller said. "This is no time to stir up dead fires."

McKinney opened his mouth as if to say something else, but he kept silent.

"For what it's worth, Joby, I don't hold with what Millpas said to you."

"He was dead wrong, Tom."

"All our nerves is rubbed plumb raw, I reckon."

Joby looked at the people who were still part of the posse and shook his head.

"It looks like you've lost most of your posse, Tom. You don't have to go on with this, either. It's going to be a long ride."

"I figure we can catch up with them tomorrow or next day, Joby. Even to me, their tracks look fresh."

"Popper still has some tricks left in his bag, Tom."

"I'll give it another few days."

"I'm going to stay with it until we catch that bastard," McKinney said. "Until I kill him and his men with my bare hands."

Joby drew in a quick breath and stared at McKinney.

"You'll probably be the first one ZP picks off, McKinney."

"You'd like that, wouldn't you, Redmond?" McKinney's face swelled and turned a reddish hue. The anger in him was very close to the surface.

"No, I hope nobody else gets killed," Joby said, "but I know Popper and I know the men with him. He won't be easy to catch."

McKinney snorted.

"And," Joby said, "he sure as hell won't be easy to kill."

"He's as good as dead already," McKinney said.

"Be careful where you walk, McKinney," Joby said.

"Huh? What do you mean by that?"

Joby looked at Keller and then at McKinney.

"Because you might just step on your own foolish grave," Joby said.

24

After supper, Joby sat with Dolores, who was sitting under a tree, her dulcimer on her lap. Mark and Forrest walked over and sat, too, their bellies full, their weariness evident in the way they slumped, their legs folded in front of them as if for support.

"Is it all right if I play, Joby?"

"Sure, Do. If you feel like it."

"I feel like playing. Maybe singing a little. It takes my mind off of the bad things that have happened."

"Then it's all right."

"Yes, Auntie Dolores," Forrest said. "Please play."

"Please," Mark said. "Like you used to play for Ma and us and for Grandma and Grandpa."

"I've been playing the dulcymore all day in my mind," she said. "Mostly sad songs. Songs in mountain minor. I just feel like playing. I need to hear the music. I need to feel it go through me, through my skin. Through my mind."

Joby said nothing. He looked at his sister and saw the sadness in her eyes, the way the firelight shifted the shadows on her face. She looked like a young Madonna just then, like a wooden carving that had come to life. Keller and the others were still sitting by the fire, except for Theodore and Keith who were on watch, circling the camp with their rifles. He could hear the crunch of their boots and saw them as occasional shadows when the light from the fire caught them in its vagrant beams.

Dolores began to pluck the dulcimer, slowly at first, as if finding her way to the music, to a particular song that was just out of reach. She sighed and let out a breath, and then her hair fell over her face as she bent over and picked out the melody line of *Red River Valley*. She played it very slowly, just the single notes, and the music floated on the night air and seemed to echo the sadness in their hearts. Then she began to add the chords and, finally, began to sing the words in a low, sweet voice.

When Dolores finished the song, there were a few moments of silence. Joby felt tears welling up in his eyes, but he did not try to stop their flow. He was thinking of his mother and father just then, remembering when they had crossed the Red River so many years before. He missed them terribly at that moment. He and Dolores exchanged glances, and then she spoke.

"That's too sad," she said. "But I had to get the sadness out of me. I felt today as if I were riding in darkness, even though the sun was shining."

"I was missing our ma all day," Mark said.

"I miss her, too," Forrest said, and Joby saw that there were tears in the eyes of both boys.

"Let me liven things up a little to change the mood," Dolores said and began picking *Bile 'em Cabbage Down.* The boys and Joby started moving their feet in time with the music. Then Dolores swung into another lively number that sounded like an Irish jig.

Those men sitting by the campfire all got up and

strolled over. They sat down in a semicircle facing Dolores. She smiled at them.

"You play a pretty fair dulcymore," Roland said. "My grandma'am used to play one, I remember."

"Mighty nice," Keller said.

McKinney scowled. He was sitting some few feet away from the others as if he had come over to listen to the music against his will.

"I don't know how you people can sit around listening to music while that bastard Popper is holding my daughter, maybe doing something bad to her."

"Oh, come on, Bill," Keller said. "We can't do anything about that tonight."

"It just don't seem proper to me," McKinney said.

"We're just as sad as you, Mr. McKinney," Dolores said. "We just all handle sadness differently, that's all. I miss my dead mother and my sister-in-law, too. But, I know I can't do anything to help either one of them right now."

The other men murmured their assent and nodded their heads in agreement.

"The music helps, Do," Joby said, and he rose to his feet and walked away. "Keep on playing as long as you like. I'll hear you."

Mark and Forrest looked each other, wondering if they should join their father. Mark started to rise and Forrest shook his head. Dolores began to pluck the dulcimer, and the tune she played was *Amazing Grace.* Then she started singing and Keller joined in first, then the others, all except McKinney, who hung his head in gloomy dejection.

Joby walked down the creek, listening to its quiet music, an undertone to the sweet sound of the dulcimer. He looked up at the big Texas sky, scanning the expanse of shimmering silver stars sparkling in a black velvet sea.

He built a smoke, struck a match and lit it, watched the

flame die away, then tossed the stick into the creek. He drew in the smoke and let it out as he faced skyward. The smoke drifted upward and then wafted into shreds as the slight evening breeze caught it. He thought of Felicia, somewhere out there, under those same stars, the moon just clearing the horizon like some great shining bone. He wondered if she was fighting off Popper or one of the other men, or sitting by herself, crying, perhaps trying to comfort Veronica McKinney, who was also weeping.

The images tore at him and gripped his throat in a strangling vise. He felt so helpless just then, with all horse tracks invisible to him, and Popper gloating over his bloody victories, swaggering about his camp, planning his next moves.

Joby told himself he should have seen all this coming. He should have taken precautions to protect his family just in case Popper broke out of prison. But he hadn't, and he had thought that Popper would never breathe free air again, that he would always be behind bars, where he belonged.

He could almost smell Felicia's fragrance on the night air, mingled with the cigarette smoke, like crushed lilacs, and the musk of tobacco on his lips when he kissed her. And the taste of flowers on her lips, that aroma of honeysuckle in her hair. He wished he was holding her in his arms now, holding her close to him, tasting the sweetness on her lips, feeling the softness of her breasts pressing against his bare chest. The longing in him grew as he closed his eyes and bowed his head as if trying to send his thoughts to her across the miles. He could almost feel the nearness of her as he sometimes did when he was out in the field working cattle or sitting on a stump hunting deer all by himself. He believed that Felicia could sometimes hear those thoughts, for she had told him more than once that she had sensed him near her, sensed him talking to her when he was not at home, but off by himself.

"Lord, I do love her so," he whispered and then opened his eyes and looked up, once again, at the stars, as if they, too, understood his deepest thoughts, his love for his wife, the terrible ache in his heart.

"I'm coming, sweetheart," he whispered. "I'm coming to get you."

He turned and looked back at the campfire and beyond, where Dolores was playing the dulcimer, with the men gathered around her in an arc of bodies, and the ache in him deepened until he felt the sting of tears welling up in his eyes.

Dolores finished playing *Lisa Jane* and then the music stopped. Joby saw her stand up and put her dulcimer back in its canvas sack. The others got up, too. He heard Keller thank her and Roland tell her how much he enjoyed her playing and her singing. His sons saw him and walked away from the others, toward him.

Joby wiped his sleeve across his eyes to dry the tears on his face. He puffed on his cigarette and waited.

"Pa, whatcha doin'?" Mark asked as he and Forrest came up.

"Just thinking. Looking at the stars."

"They're mighty pretty," Forrest said, looking up.

He sounded sad, Joby thought.

"It's a nice evening," Joby said.

"It would be, if Ma was with us," Mark said. "I could hardly stand it when Auntie Dolores was singing some of those songs."

"They made me real sad," Forrest said.

Joby continued smoking his cigarette, watching the smoke drift skyward and turn to ghostly wisps.

"Pa, why is living life so hard?" Mark had turned serious all of a sudden. "I mean, why can't it just be nice and easy like it used to be?"

"Like it is sometimes," Forrest said. "It's hard now, without Ma and with Granny gone forever."

Joby took a last puff and let his cigarette drop to the earth. He ground it out with the heel of his boot. He expelled the smoke in his lungs.

"Living," Joby said, "is what we do every day. Life is what happens to you along the way."

"I don't understand," Mark said.

"Me, neither." Forrest stepped closer, as if eager to hear what his father had to say.

"I've thought about it some," Joby said. "Life. And living."

"And?" Mark pressed him.

"Life seems to me like some kind of journey, boys. It's something you've got to get through and you can't see very far ahead. And when something goes wrong, that's kind of like a test, maybe an obstacle in your path. You've got to get around it, or over it, or through it, and each time you do, you learn a little bit more. And, I think, if you can, you're supposed to teach someone else what you learned along the way."

"Who?" Forrest asked.

"Maybe you, and Mark, and Auntie Dolores. Maybe anyone you love or are responsible for."

"What's the purpose of doing all that?" Mark asked. "I guess I mean what's the purpose of life, of going through all that?"

"Good question," Joby said. "I don't know. I don't think anybody knows. But I think life has a purpose or else why are we living it?"

"Life stinks," Mark said.

"Yeah," Forrest said. "It's not fair. It's not fair what happened to Granny and Ma and those people, Mr. Cherry and his family."

"Life can beat you, if you let it," Joby said. "You can either learn from it, or suffer from it."

"We're learning, all right," Forrest said, "and suffering from it."

"Pain is a pretty good teacher, boys." Joby looked over and saw that Keller and the others were crawling into their bedrolls. His sister was sitting by the fire, looking his way. He turned his head. He didn't want her to come over. If she did, he figured they'd have to start the conversation all over again and be up all night.

"I don't understand none of it," Mark said.

"In time, you will," Joby said.

"Understand what?" Forrest asked.

"Why you're here and what you're supposed to do. Just don't sit on the porch and whittle when you get old. Keep looking. Keep thinking. Keep learning."

"I've already learned enough, Pa."

"Have you? Then maybe you should just ride on back home and let someone else make your journey. We're going after your ma. We're going to bring her back home."

"And we're going to teach that Popper a lesson, I reckon," Forrest said.

"We are," Joby said.

"If you put it that way . . ." Forrest said.

"If you quit, Forrest, you're still learning a lesson. If you go on when you want to quit, you're learning a different lesson. One might help you go the rest of the way, the other might not."

"Huh?"

"Whatever gets in your path, you've got to get past. If you don't, you might have to walk that way again and it won't be as easy the second time."

"I reckon you've learned a lot, Pa," Forrest said.

"Not nearly enough," Joby said.

Then he smiled as he looked at his sons.

"Let's get some shut-eye. We're going to get an early morning start tomorrow."

"On the journey?" Mark said.

Joby nodded.

"It never quits," he said. "And neither will I."

25

Joby put his hand on the sheriff's shoulder and shook him gently. Keller's eyes batted open and closed, then remained open.

"Redmond? That you?" When the sheriff spoke, his breath reeked of alcohol. Joby smelled it and was taken aback by the strong odor of whiskey. He hadn't seen Keller take a drink the night before. So Joby thought that he must be a secret drinker. The worst kind, in his experience.

"Tom, Johnny and I are riding out. Nobody's on watch. Everybody's asleep."

"Hellfire, it's still dark as pitch out."

"There's some light in the sky. Enough for us to see. But you got weather comin' in."

"Huh?" Keller sat up, rubbed his eyes. He looked around as Joby stood up.

"We're goin' to get some rain and that'll wipe out all the tracks for sure. So, Johnny and I have got to light a shuck. Get everybody up and follow close."

"Are we a-goin' to lose them jaspers?"

"I've got a pretty good idea where they're headed, Tom.

You leave that to me. There's weather comin' up from the Gulf and it's goin' to hit us before noon. I'll be seein' ya."

Joby walked a few paces away where Johnny waited on his horse, holding the reins of Joby's mount. Joby did not look back at Keller, but mounted and headed for the road. Roland rode at his side.

"Did you tell him about the storm, Joby?"

"He'll know soon enough. That light in the east is going to close up like a trapdoor pretty quick."

"That's for sure. You hungry, Joby?"

"I never like to eat when I'm huntin'," Joby said. "I'll chew on some jerky in an hour or so. I want to get a good look at those tracks and see where Popper made camp last night."

"I get the feelin' that he wasn't all that far ahead of us."

"Me, too," Joby said as he rode through the predawn shadows over a road that was occasionally overgrown, and yielded few tracks in the dimness of the fading night.

He had taken the last watch with Roland so that they could both saddle up and get moving when it was light enough to see. He was relieved that none of Popper's men had doubled back and shot any of them. It was something that Popper had done before and it had been a worry all the long night.

There had been a shift in the breeze during the night and he had felt a change of weather coming in. If it rained, and he was sure that it would, he knew that Popper's tracks would be wiped out and it might take days before he could pick up the outlaw's trail again.

But he figured that by leaving early, he might steal a march on Popper, gain some ground on him before the rain hit. He knew, though, that ZP was not going to stick to the old road for very much longer. Right now, he figured the bunch was headed for Fort Worth, and from there, they could either keep heading westward, or cut south or north.

When Joby had caught up with Popper before and put him and his men in prison, ZP had taunted him about having a hideout that nobody would ever find and that if he'd had a few more days, he would have gotten to it and escaped capture.

It might have been idle boasting, but Joby had learned to listen to what men said and the way they said things. Popper was a boaster, but underneath Joby had sensed an underlying truth. The man had a past, after all, and he had roamed all over Texas in his younger days. In particular, west Texas.

"I got me a place in the wild," Popper had said. "A little shanty where I can crawl into my hole and pull the hole right in after me. Even a damned Apache couldn't find me."

That's what the man had said, and now Joby was thinking about that particular boast. But Texas was a big place and west Texas could be a hell for a man not used to wind and dust and emptiness. When he had caught up with Popper, that seemed to be where he was headed, just like he had said. But where? And how much further would Joby have had to track him? How far west was Popper going? To the New Mexico border, or maybe just out to the Palo Duro where a man could crawl into a hole and pull it in after him. Wild. Wild places. Places where a man could go mad in the sun or suffocate in the winds that blew down from the north and carried dirt and dust clear from New Mexico, Colorado and Wyoming.

The light slowly seeped in behind them, but ahead there were only dark bulging clouds and a wind that scoured their faces and brought gusts that tasted of rain. Joby saw the tracks of his quarry appear as if by magic, a tangle of hieroglyphic scrawls that his practiced eye began to decipher. He separated the tracks in his mind and measured the distance between fore and hind hooves, the way the shoes struck the ground.

"These are last night's tracks," Joby said, "and ZP was pushing his horses at a pretty fair clip."

"Too fast for them to hold up long. I expect we'll find where they made camp pretty quick."

"No telling how long they rode at this pace, but my guess is that after they crossed the creek where we camped last night, that's when they put spurs to their horseflesh."

"I'm countin' hours," Roland said.

"Yes. Less than half a day, I reckon."

"No way to tell until we find where they put up for the night and then see how fresh this morning's hoofprints are."

Roland nodded and turned his attention back to the road and the maze of tracks heading westward. Joby did the same, a small worry in his mind that was beginning to build as the wind blew freshets of air against his face and he listened for the distant sound of thunder.

An hour later, the tracks left the road and both men examined the trampled grasses, the overturned stones that marked the path Popper and his men had taken. They rode more slowly now, but so had Popper. Yet Joby got the feeling that ZP knew exactly where he was going. He seemed to have slowed just to let the horses blow and catch a second wind.

A half mile off the road, deep in a thick stand of pines and cedars, oaks and hickories, Roland reined up at a place where the grass had been chewed on, and where there were flattened and dry places where bedrolls appeared to have been laid out, untouched by the morning dew.

"This looks like the place where they bedded down, Joby."

" 'Pears to be," Joby said. He fished for the makings and rolled a quirlie. He offered the sack to Johnny. Johnny took it and began build a smoke.

The two men rode around the campsite, searching for any sign that might help them later on. It had been a dry camp, no fire, and it appeared they all had left just after the dew had settled on the ground around dawn. A good sign, Joby thought.

"We're not far behind them, Johnny."

"Nope. Couple of hours, maybe."

"Less than three, I figure."

"No sign of the women."

"At least they're still alive," Joby said.

"Would Popper kill them?"

"If they slowed him down, he would."

Roland swore.

The two men finished their cigarettes shortly after they took up the trail once more and they kept their horses at a brisk pace, trying to close the gap between themselves and the outlaws. The morning turned darker as they rode and Joby kept looking at the sky, wondering when it would open up and drench the land, obliterating all the tracks, all traces of Popper and his gang, and their two women captives.

"Somethin' up ahead," Roland said, breaking into Joby's thoughts. He pointed at a large dark hulk that was half on the road, half in the grass to the side.

"Uh-oh," Joby said.

"I'm going to ride up for a look-see."

"Better wait, Johnny. I think I know what it is."

"What?"

"It looks like a dead horse."

"I'll find out," Roland said, before Joby could stop him. He held up an arm as if to hold Roland back, but Johnny was already galloping ahead.

"Johnny," Joby called, slipping his rifle from its scabbard. "Wait."

Several thoughts fought for supremacy in Joby's mind as he brought his rifle out and thumbed the hammer back. First of all, the road was straight for a long way, something that was unusual in that part of the country where roads twisted and curved like meandering streams. If that was a dead horse, he was pretty sure that it hadn't died of old age. And the third thing that bothered him was that both sides of the road were thick with timber, offering concealment as far as the eye could see. It was just such a place, Joby knew, that ZP would have chosen for an ambush if he knew he outnumbered his pursuers. That dead horse hadn't just picked that particular place to lie down and die. Somebody had put it right there, where it could attract attention and be seen for a long way with an unobstructed view.

Joby didn't like any of it, and he had failed to stop Roland from riding straight at the horse hell bent for leather.

"Damn," Joby said, squinting his eyes, looking for any sign of movement on either side of the road. He was looking for a flash of color, a jiggling leaf, anything out of place. The darkness of the day limited his vision, but he could see well enough.

Nothing seemed out of place.

But he knew it was no accident that they had come upon a dead horse in the middle of the road. In the middle of a dangerous road. Roland was exposed. He was out in the open and had no cover.

As Joby was thinking these thoughts, he gently nudged his horse forward, but tugged on the reins so that the animal sidled along, giving Joby a clear view of the dead horse, and the roadway ahead.

He kept the horse at a slow walk, his rifle at the ready.

Johnny reined up at the dead horse, then turned and faced Joby.

"It's a dead horse all right. I seen it in town. It's one of them—"

And that was all Roland was able to say.

A single rifle shot cracked in the gloomy stillness, sounding like the crack of a bullwhip.

Joby's heart froze in his chest. He looked at Johnny, but his eyes were also looking for a flash in the trees. For a long moment, he thought Roland had escaped being hit by a bullet. The sound of the shot died in the air and an eerie quiet descended on the road.

Joby listened for rustling, or hoofbeats, but heard nothing.

Roland raised a hand in the air as if waving hello, or good-bye, and then crumpled in the saddle. He fell to the ground like a sack of meal and Joby knew it was going to be bad. The impact of the bullet had not caused Roland to jerk or twitch, so it must have hit a vital organ. Joby had seen deer run for a hundred yards or more with a fatal shot to the heart.

That's what it looked like, from the way Roland acted following the shot. Like a man caught by death when he wasn't near ready to die.

"Johnny," Joby called, hoping against all hope that Roland was still alive. "Hold on."

Joby had not seen a flash, but he had heard the shot clearly and knew from what direction it had come. He scanned the underbrush, the trees, the left side of the road. The shooter was somewhere in there, or had been. He might even be lining up his sights at that very moment, fixing to drop Joby with another shot.

Joby clucked to his horse and headed off the road, to the right, keeping his eyes on the road ahead, beyond where Roland lay, and on the woods to his left. He held his breath as if expecting it to be his last.

Johnny was not moving. Joby reached the shelter of the trees and faded into the underbrush. The silence grew up around him like some cloaking shroud, enveloping him, nearly blotting out all other senses, smothering his thoughts in a solemn dark tomb in which all reality had vanished as if somewhere nearby, the last candle on earth had been snuffed out, plunging the world into a soundless darkness, a world bereft of all life, except his own.

26

THEN THE DEEP SILENCE WAS BROKEN BY THE FAINT RUMBLE of distant thunder. Joby let out the breath he had been holding so long he thought his lungs were on fire. There was life on earth after all, he thought.

But there was also death, and it was waiting out there for him just as surely as that faraway thunder proclaimed that a storm was coming.

Joby rode on, through the woods, paralleling the road, the stand of timber on the other side. He drew closer to the place where Johnny Roland lay so still and unmoving, his horse standing a few feet away, hipshot, half asleep, as if waiting for his master to mount him once again.

Joby stopped as he passed the place where Roland lay in the road. He stopped and listened for a long time. Then, as he was about to move again, he heard something, something that he at first could not identify.

Hoofbeats. The ragged thrum of hoofbeats on the road beyond. Clear and distinct now. Joby jabbed his spurs into his horse's flanks and shot through the trees to the fringe of grass bordering the road. In the distance, he saw a lone rider flogging his horse with the tips of his reins, bent over the saddle, riding fast. Joby pulled his rifle to his shoulder and cocked the hammer back as it seated. He laid the front blade sight on the fleeing man, and lined it up with the rear buckhorn. Then he elevated the barrel, judging the speed and distance of the horse, then held his breath. He squeezed the trigger and felt the butt of the rifle recoil against his shoulder. He let the rifle barrel dip and looked at horse and rider to see if he had struck either one.

The man looked back over his shoulder and then continued on. Joby knew he had missed. A moment later, the outlaw disappeared and Joby waited a few seconds, listening to the faint sound of retreating hoofbeats.

Then it was silent once again.

Joby sighed and brought his rifle down. He dug another .44/70 cartridge out of his pocket and stuffed it into the chamber, then slid the rifle back into its scabbard.

He rode back to where Roland lay facedown in the road, spoke to Johnny's horse, then dismounted, leaving his horse ground-tied.

"Johnny?" Joby said, as he walked over to Roland.

Roland let out a low groan.

Joby knelt down beside the stricken man and looked at him. There was blood staining Roland's shirt at the small of his back, and a neat black hole right in the center near the base of the spine. Joby saw splintered pieces of bone inside the hole when he bent over for a closer look.

The shooter must have waited up the road so that he could shoot Roland in the back. Sneaky, Joby thought. He dreaded turning Roland over and seeing the exit wound. But perhaps the bullet had deflected, or remained somewhere inside Roland's body.

Joby leaned over and spoke into Roland's ear.

"Johnny," he said. "Can you hear me?"

Roland groaned again. The sound startled Joby and he jerked backward involuntarily.

"Can you move?"

"Don't feel nothin'. Am I dead?"

"You're alive, but you took the bullet in your backbone, Johnny. I'm going to turn you over. Let me know if there's too much pain."

"Unh," Johnny muttered.

Joby looked at the back wound one more time. The edge was ragged on one side where the bone had splintered. This could have been caused either by the shattered bone or the bullet, or both, he thought.

"Grit your teeth, Johnny."

Joby shifted his position to a squat and reached both arms under Roland's body, one at the legs, the other at the chest. These were the strongest points and would cause the least pain and damage when he turned the wounded man over. He lifted, grunting with the effort, and gingerly turned Roland over on his side. Then he took away his left hand and set it atop Johnny's legs to steady him. Next, he withdrew his right hand from where it had lain under Roland's chest and put it on his side, just beneath the armpit. He stood up and straddled Johnny, then eased him onto his back.

"Did that hurt, Johnny?"

"Unh-unh."

"Let me take a look at you. If I hurt you, just yell out."

Roland did not say anything.

Gently, Joby laid Roland on his back. Johnny did not even groan, but let out a weak sigh. There was no blood on the front of his shirt where the exit wound should have been had the bullet gone clear through him.

Joby felt around Roland's midsection and looked on both sides of his body, but could detect no wound.

"Can you talk, Johnny?"

"Damned little."

"You've got a hole in your back, right at the bottom of your backbone. The bullet didn't come out your front or sides. It may still be inside you, or it may have deflected off somewhere. That hole, where it is, might be why you don't have any feeling in your legs. Can you move 'em?"

Roland seemed to be struggling to move his legs. Sweat beaded up on his forehead. He grunted and relaxed.

"Did they move?" he asked.

Joby shook his head.

"I've got some pain back there," Roland said. "But it seems like it's far away. Sharp sometimes. Dull at others. I feel real funny. My head feels like it's full of lint or maybe cotton fuzz."

"Do you want a drink of water?"

"I could use a drink of something."

Joby got the canteen from Johnny's horse and brought it to him. He held Roland's head up and poured a small amount of water past his lips. When Roland nodded that he was finished, Joby recorked the wooden canteen and set it down beside the wounded man.

"I'm going to pull you off the road and we'll wait for Keller and the others to catch up."

"Do you trust Keller?" Roland asked.

"Should I?"

"He was mighty eager to draw up a posse. And he picked men he knew wouldn't give him no trouble."

"Like McKinney?"

"He didn't want McKinney. But he couldn't get out of it."

"So, that's how I'd pick a posse, maybe," Joby said.

"When some of those jaspers come into the saloon, they acted like they knew Tom."

"Did they speak to him?"

"No, but it was like they knew him."

"The badge, maybe."

"Nope, it wasn't that. I mean it wasn't that they seemed to know who he was. It was like they knew him."

"What made you think that?"

"Just the way they looked at him. Real quick and then Popper, he turned away, and I caught a smirk on his face when he did that. The others, too, they hardly noticed that there was a sheriff there. And a bunch of owlhoots bound for robbin' a bank just don't act thataway. Not to my mind, they don't."

"You might have a point there, Johnny."

Joby got up and grabbed Roland under his armpits. He dragged his limp body off the road and lay it in the grass that grew alongside. Roland never complained. Joby lifted him in such a way that his wound was off the ground. He walked back to the horses and took Johnny's bedroll off the saddle and brought it over. He folded it up and put it under Roland's head.

"Thanks, Joby."

Joby nodded and then walked back and brought the canteen over. He held it up and Roland shook his head. Joby set it down near him, then went after the two horses. He led them back and tied them to some small, young trees.

He was thinking about what Roland had said about Tom Keller. Tom could have been in on the bank robbery, of course. One of the clerks was, and who knew how many others saw a way to make some easy money? If Keller was in on it, then, by leading the posse, he would make sure that they never caught up with Popper. But then, how would Keller get his share of the bank loot? That was something he'd have to find out and it would not be easy.

If Keller was part of the scheme to rob the bank in Gilmet, he had covered his tracks well. Joby didn't remember anyone named Keller in the Second Texas. But, of course, he hadn't known everyone in the outfit. Maybe Keller had changed his name, or maybe he had met Popper after ZP had deserted the outfit and gone on the outlaw trail.

Joby realized that all he had were questions and more questions. As for Roland speaking up at this time, that was nothing new to Joby. He had heard a deathbed confession or two during the war. Maybe Roland thought he was dying and had to get something off his chest. Otherwise, why had he waited until now to speak up about his suspicions about Sheriff Keller?

"Johnny," Joby said, when he returned to Roland's side, "why did Keller pick you for his posse?"

"He knew Millpas and I were friends. Bob wouldn't have rode out with Tom less'n I was along."

"Is that all? What about Millpas? Is he part of it, too?"

"I don't think so."

"Where did Keller come from? How long has he lived in Gilmet?"

"He come there after the war. He said he had sheriffed before and he got elected after someone killed the sheriff they had before him."

"Someone killed the previous sheriff? Who?"

"He was bushwhacked. Nobody never found out who done it."

"What was the name of the sheriff before Keller?"

"Kirby. Kirby Henley. He was a good ol' boy, I reckon."

Joby ran the name through his mind. He had known a Henley in the Second Texas. But he couldn't remember if his first name was Kirby or not. Not just then. But the name struck another chord.

"Was he any relation to Georgia Henley? She works at the bank."

"Yeah, that's right. Kirby was her son."

"Did he fight in the war?"

"Yeah, I believe he did. He come back after it was over

and got himself elected sheriff right off. He was mighty nervous all the time, though. Like he was always lookin' over his shoulder. I guess he had good reason."

"He might have known ZP."

"Then why kill him that way?"

"Maybe he wouldn't do what Popper wanted him to, I reckon. Maybe Keller would."

"I saw him the day he was killed. I mean I saw him during the day and he was shot that night. He looked like somebody had punched him in the stomach. Kinda sickly lookin', he was. He had been gone a couple of days and when he come back he didn't look too good."

"Did he go into the bank that day?"

"Why, yeah, Joby, he did. He looked even sicker when he come out."

Joby was beginning to form a picture of what might have happened to Kirby and why Keller might be involved with Popper. Popper had probably wanted him to set up the bank job and Kirby had backed out because his mother worked there. He probably talked to Elmer Reynolds about it and told Reynolds he wanted no part of it. Reynolds must have gotten word to Popper who had Henley murdered. Popper was a man who planned things way ahead of time.

"Were Kirby and Elmer Reynolds friends?"

"Yeah, they were. Elmer felt real bad when Kirby got killed."

"I'll bet he did," Joby said.

He could see that Roland was tiring and he already had more than enough information to mull over for the next several days. He offered Johnny some water and Roland drank, then lay back down and closed his eyes.

The thunder sounded closer than before and the day was turning darker by the moment. Joby walked over and stood under the trees and rolled a quirly. He smoked in the deep silence, listening to the thunder. After a while, he could see lightning flashes to the west. He started timing them with the sound of thunder. He figured the storm was a good twenty miles off and moving slowly.

The storm was nothing like the one in his mind, though. And wound all through his thoughts was the vision of his wife, Felicia, and he wondered how she was faring with Popper on such a dark day. His heart felt as if it were being squeezed when he thought of her.

By the time he finished his cigarette, he saw Keller and the rest of the posse approaching. For a moment, the thought crossed his mind to kill Keller when he rode up. But he had no proof, and he was neither judge nor jury.

Still, the thought crossed his mind, as fleeting as one of those brilliant and lethal flashes of lightning.

27

As Sheriff Keller and the rag-tag posse approached, Joby kept one eye on the western skies as if to make sure that the storm stayed away a little while longer. Lightning laced the bulging black clouds, stitching ragged mercury latticework into the dark backdrop.

The wind was building and he heard it rattle through the trees like grapeshot, making great whooshing sounds and ripping leaves from the tree limbs, bending the saplings until they seemed like dervishes caught up in some drug-induced dance.

Keller was bent over, holding his hat brim down over his face to lessen the shock of the stinging wind, and those that followed him were also bent over their pommels like mendicants in prayer, their clothes flapping against their bodies, fluffing out and collapsing like wind-whipped sails in a wild gale.

"What in hell happened here?" Keller growled, his voice raspy from whiskey. Joby smelled the fumes from three feet away.

"Johnny got shot," Joby said.

"The hell you say." Keller swung down from his horse and walked over to where Johnny lay, leading his horse by the loose reins. "Johnny? You all right?"

"He needs a surgeon, Tom. He's got a bullet hole in his backbone."

"Damn."

The others rode to the fringe of the woods and dismounted, tying their horses to saplings and bushes. Lightning scored the clouds and thunder boomed a dozen miles away. The wind picked up speed and energy and leaves flew like drunken bats out of the woods. Pine needles rattled and branches swayed in ragged rhythms, creaking under the strain of the gusts.

The sky darkened even more as the black clouds surged toward and over them all like some portent of evil to come, or evil already visited upon them.

"He looks done for to me," Keller said, his tongue thick with drink.

"He's not done for, Keller. You've got to take him back to Gilmet. Doc Anderecky can patch him up."

"I got to stay on the track after Popper." Keller walked away from Roland, listing to one side as if he were on the rolling deck of a ship.

"In a half hour or so, there won't be a track to follow. You and your posse rig up a travois and carry Johnny back to town."

Keller looked at Joby as if surprised by the authority in Joby's voice.

"I'm in charge here."

"Not anymore, you aren't."

"What in hell's that supposed to mean, Redmond?"

"It means your job is over here. As far as I'm concerned you're just a field ambulance."

"Be damned if I am. You can't give me orders."

The others, hearing the higher pitch in Keller's voice,

began to drift over to the two men. They formed a half circle. Dolores looked at Roland and walked over to him, knelt down and took his hand. The boys stood on shifting feet, looking at their father's face.

"You don't have any jurisdiction out here, Keller. If you think you can last another week or two, or a month, then you go right ahead and stay after Popper. But if Johnny doesn't get to a sawbones, he's going to die."

"If he dies, he dies," Keller said.

"You bastard," Joby said. "You aren't fit to wear that badge."

Keller stepped back a foot. His right hand hovered above his holstered pistol.

"Tom, don't do nothin' foolish," Keith said.

"This is no time for gunplay," Theodore said quickly. He walked over to Keller and grabbed his forearm, the one that was attached to Keller's gun hand.

"Damn you, Redmond." Keller's mouth was liquid with spittle.

"You take that hogleg out of its pouch, Keller, and it'll be the last thing you ever do," Joby said.

"Are you threatening me? An officer of the law?"

"You know your own boot size. See if it fits, Keller."

"I ought to put you in irons, Redmond, take you back to jail."

"You're welcome to try."

Keller balled up his fists in a defiant gesture. He looked, for a moment, as if he were about to step forward and try to take Joby into custody, but he evidently thought better of it and just stood there, fuming with rage.

"You ever come back to Gilmet, I'll arrest you, Redmond. You can bank on that."

"You're the expert on banking, Keller."

"What in hell do you mean by that crack?"

"I think you know something about that bank job."

Keller's face reddened and his neck muscles swelled and bulged like a bull's in the rut. He opened his mouth to say something, but Gordon Keith stepped forward then and put himself between Keller and Joby.

"Tom, don't get yourself in a dither," Keith said. "We've got us a wounded man yonder who needs to see Doc Anderecky. I think Joby's right. There's a storm blowin' in that's going to wipe out all horse tracks. I think we've done our part. It's time to fold our hand and get out of the game."

"He's right, Tom," William Theodore said. "We're going to get mighty wet pretty quick. And it's a long ride back to Gilmet. Let's pack it up. You and Redmond can settle your differences later."

"Johnny's going to die if we don't get him to the doctor's soon," Dolores said. "He's lost blood and he looks mighty puny to me."

Everyone looked at Dolores and the stricken Roland.

"I'll help you boys cut some saplings to make a travois," Joby said. "Get some rope and we'll rig Johnny a litter you can pull behind your horses."

Keller glared at Joby one more time and then muttered something under his breath. He turned away and walked over to Roland, then looked down at him. Dolores stood up and moved away.

"We're going to take you back to town, Johnny," Keller said. "You just hold on, hear?"

Roland batted his eyes, but he said nothing.

Joby, the other two men, and Forrest and Mark all went into the woods to cut some slender trees down. In a half hour, Joby had rigged a travois.

Keller, Joby, Keith and Theodore all lifted Roland up and placed him next to the makeshift litter, which Joby had tested for its strength before approving it for travel.

Joby walked over and led Roland's horse to the front of

the travois. He unwrapped the thongs around the bedroll, shook out Johnny's slicker and handed it to Dolores.

"Get the boys to help you, Do. Put this on Johnny, will you?"

"Mark, Forrest, give me a hand," Dolores said.

"Keith, get that other side pole and run it through the stirrup," Joby said. "I'll do this side. Let's do it together."

The two men lifted the poles and pulled the travois up so that the side poles straddled Roland's horse. They slid the pole ends through the stirrups.

"Theodore, give Keith a hand," Joby said. "Lash that pole up good. We don't want it to break loose on the ride back."

Both men nodded and began to hitch the travois pole to the saddle rings, as Joby instructed them on what to do. Lightning danced a few miles away and the thunder was now deafening as Keller, Keith and Theodore started to mount up.

Joby tested the lashings on both poles. He pulled and stretched each pole to see that they were seated solidly and securely.

Dolores and Joby's sons finished slipping Roland into his slicker. They stood beside him.

"Joby," Roland called, his voice very weak.

"Yeah?"

"I got that pain you was askin' about. It's all over, like fire."

"Where?"

"In my back and up to my shoulders."

"Maybe Keller will give you some of his whiskey."

Keller turned when he heard his name mentioned.

"What's that?" Keller asked.

"Can you spare Johnny here some of your whiskey? He's feeling the bite of that bullet," Joby said.

"I don't have no whiskey."

"Well, you may find some when Johnny starts screamin'," Joby said.

Keller turned away, his face as sullen as the black sky above.

"Let's lift Johnny on to the travvy," Joby said to Gordon and Theodore. He looked at McKinney, who was sliding into his raincoat and stood well away from the activity.

"McKinney, you go on back, too," Joby said. He had noticed that McKinney had been trying to be invisible during the argument and the rigging of the travois.

"Like hell I am."

"You get his shoulder, Keith," Joby said. "Theodore you lift this shoulder. I'll take his feet. Gently now."

The three men lifted Roland up and laid him on the travois.

"Now, lash him up," Joby said. "Not too tight, but tight enough to keep him from rolling off."

"It hurts real bad, Joby," Roland said.

"That's a sign you're still alive, Johnny. I wish I had something to give you."

"I know. I'll just grit it on out."

Joby smiled. He knew bravery when he saw it. Roland was made of the right stuff.

Joby went over to his horse and worked his slicker loose. He put it on and saw that his sons and his sister were doing the same.

"I don't want you with us," Joby said, walking over to McKinney.

"I go where you go, Redmond."

"Well, if you get hurt, we'll have to leave you."

"I'll keep up."

Keller and the others started to move out. Keith and Theodore both held on to a rein from Roland's horse. They turned and waved good-bye, following Keller. Keller did not turn around, but set off at a trot, heading back to Gilmet. The yellow slickers disappeared around a bend of the road and what was left of the posse was gone.

"Ready, Do?" Joby asked.

She nodded.

"We may have to take shelter pretty quick, but let's start out. That lightning's getting mighty close."

"Too close," Forrest said as the sky lit up and thunder pealed loudly two or three seconds later.

They all mounted up and started riding westward.

Five minutes later, rain began to sting their faces and then the wind surged and the rain came at them like millions of silver lances. The water blinded them and Joby led them off the road and into a copse of trees that offered some, but very little, protection.

"We'll hole up here for a time," Joby said. "Stay away from the trees. Get under your horses and hunker down."

He had to yell to make himself heard as the thunder crashed and lightning streaked the sky and skewered silvery lancets into the ground.

There they all waited, watching the land light up as if from a photographer's phosphorous explosions. The rain came down in steady heavy sheets and they could hear water running somewhere like a lost river come to life, come to carry away the dead and the dying left from the battle raging in the heavens.

28

JOBY LINED UP THE FIVE HORSES BELONGING TO HIM AND HIS family and Bill McKinney, and hobbled them close together. He and the others sat beneath the horses' bellies as the storm raged in full fury. Lightning slashed the skies all around them and the thunder was an almost continuous roar. Each person held onto the reins and patted the horses to calm them.

"What was all that about with the sheriff?" Dolores asked her brother during one of the rare lulls between thunderclaps. "Do you think he was in on the robbery?"

McKinney leaned closer to listen. Mark and Forrest were attentive, too.

"Johnny Roland mentioned that Keller might have been in cahoots with Popper."

"That's just awful," Dolores said. "Do you think the sheriff was in on it?"

"I don't know," Joby said. "I wouldn't put it past Popper. I don't know the sheriff that well. He could have known Popper before, though. Right now, he's the least of my worries."

"The storm, you mean."

"No. Felicia."

He wondered where she was and whether or not she was wet and cold, perhaps still on horseback, riding through the storm. That would be Popper's way. Popper did not care about other people and he was a stubborn, determined man. Popper would likely look at the storm as a boon, a way for him to put miles between himself and pursuit. He would ride his men and his prisoners into the ground and never bat an eye.

Dolores put a hand on her bother's arm and he looked at her in the dim light. Was that rain in her eyes, or was she weeping? He did not know. Perhaps both. He felt heartsick that he was unable to keep going in the storm and that he might never see his wife again. He had never felt so lonesome in his life as he did right now.

Joby and Felicia had both loved the rain and they had often sat on the porch watching it fall and soak the ground, bringing nourishment and life to the things they had planted. He thought of her now, sitting on the porch with him, listening to the patter of rain on the roof, the soft *tink* as it struck the tin gutters, the melodious sound it made as it created thousands of tiny rivers around the house and ran down the spouts in miniature torrents.

"Don't worry, Joby," Dolores whispered. "Felicia can take care of herself. She knows you're coming to get her."

"Yes," he said. "She knows."

He looked at his sons. They were huddled together under their horses like drenched birds, drenched yellow birds in their slickers. He could not see their faces, but he knew they were feeling miserable. When they were small they used to love to play in the rain, but now that they were older, they wanted to stay dry and would head for the nearest shelter the moment anything wet fell from the sky.

McKinney was the farthest away, hunkered down low

on his butt in his black slicker, the water shining on it every time lightning struck, his hat dripping where the brim stuck out from under his horse. Like me, Joby thought, he is probably thinking of his daughter, Veronica, and that bastard, Popper. Thoughts like that could eat a man alive. Thoughts like that could kill a man just as quick as poison.

In the shrieking wind, Joby thought he could hear Felicia screaming and the sound tore at his heart even though he knew it was only his imagination. His own thoughts. Bad to think them. Very bad. He tried to shake them off and he looked at his sister again. She had moved closer to him for warmth or comfort, and he put his arm around her shoulders and held her tightly against him. She shivered every time the lightning flashed and every time the thunder crashed against their eardrums like the roar of heavy cannon.

Joby knew the storm would last a long time, probably through most of the night. He knew they could not stay huddled up underneath the horses. They would have to eat and sleep, get some rest before continuing the pursuit of ZP. They were in for a wet, miserable night.

"Dolores," he said. "I'm going to build us a shelter. We have to get some rest and put the horses someplace where they can graze. You stay here with the boys. I'll cut some branches and get everything ready."

"Do you want some help?"

"When I finish cutting what we need. No use in all of us getting soaked."

She nodded and Joby crabbed out from beneath his horse. Dolores leaned over and spoke to the boys. McKinney made no sign that he knew what was going on. He remained huddled up beneath his horse, holding the collar of his slicker up over his face. His head was bent and he seemed to be locked in a world of his own.

Joby used his knife to cut pine branches from a number

of trees. He stacked them up in the midst of a small clearing between other trees, including an oak and a hickory. It was hard, wet work and he had to reach high for some of the lower branches on the taller trees. When he had finished, he began cutting and stripping some of the limbs and leaned them against trees in a triangular shape. Then he stacked the other cut branches against these frames and wound up with four small lean-tos that would keep some of the rain from them as they slept.

When he was finished he walked back to where the others were waiting and called them out.

"Unhobble your horses and follow me," he said.

Mark and Forrest both seemed eager to come out from under their horses. Dolores soon followed. McKinney still sat there, huddled over like a low-caste Indian mendicant.

"McKinney," Joby said, leaning down to talk to the man above the roar of the storm, "come on. I've got a place where you can get some sleep."

"Huh?" McKinney lifted his head and looked at Joby. He seemed dazed, and his eyes were puffy, his face blanched.

"Come on. We're moving from here."

"Oh, yeah, sure."

McKinney's voice sounded odd. Then a flash of lightning revealed McKinney's face, the red-rimmed eyes, the poached flesh. Joby realized that the man had been crying. For how long, he did not know, but the puffed eyes and the constriction in his throat both pointed to the fact that McKinney had been bawling.

Joby watched as McKinney crawled out from under his horse.

"Where we going?" he asked.

"I built some shelters. Bring your horse. We'll hobble them in another place."

"All right." McKinney seemed submissive and that was not like him, Joby knew. At least he had not been behaving that way ever since Joby had seen him ride up to his place.

Joby spoke to Dolores and the boys and pointed to where he wanted them to go. He watched them leave, leading their horses in single file through the rain-swept trees, lightning illuminating their shapes so that they seemed to appear and disappear as they walked farther and farther away from him.

Then Joby turned to McKinney, who seemed to be having trouble with his horse's hobbles.

"Need a hand?" Joby asked.

"Can't seem to get these damned hobbles off."

"Back away. I'll get it."

Joby bent down, took the hobbles off and handed them to McKinney. Lightning stormed the clouds, lacing them with a jagged silver light and splashing the ground with intense illumination.

"What's the matter, McKinney? Are you hurt?"

McKinney shook his head. He appeared dazed, confused.

"I been thinking of Ronnie. Veronica. God, I can't stand it. She's with those beasts and I'm here in this storm."

"That kind of thinking does you no good."

"I can't stop thinking of her, what those men are doing to her."

"You don't know that they're doing anything to her. Why torture yourself?"

"I can just picture her with them. Those men on top of her. Ronnie screaming. Crying. Fighting them. Getting beat up by them. Christ, I want to kill them all right now."

"You've got to get those pictures out of your mind, McKinney. They'll tear you to pieces."

"Damn it, Redmond, doesn't it bother you that your own wife is being sullied while we sit here and wait out this damned storm?"

"I don't like it any better than you do," Joby said. "But, I don't brood on it none."

"Well, you should, you heartless bastard. If that was my wife . . ."

"Well, Felicia is not your wife. You can sure worry about your daughter, like I worry about my wife, but if you keep thinking, no, imagining, what's being done to her, you'll wind up in a crazy house."

"You're a cold-blooded bastard, Redmond. As cold-blooded as those beasts who took my Ronnie."

"I think you got too much sun yesterday, McKinney. Now, get to that shelter before you drown standing up."

Joby led McKinney to the place where he had built the hasty shelters and told him to hobble his horse with the others and get out of the rain. He checked on his sons and his sister and saw that they were curled up inside the lean-tos, all dry for the moment and grateful to be out of the pounding rain.

Joby crawled into his own little shelter and leaned against the tree. He was tired, but not sleepy. McKinney's fears had worked on him, despite his resolution not to think about Felicia and what Popper and his men might be doing to her.

The hatred surged up in him, unbidden, clawing at his brain like some slavering animal and he pictured what he would do to Popper and his men when he caught up with them. And he was sure that he would catch them. There wasn't enough country in Texas or in the Union to hide them. He wished he could kill each man with his bare hands, but he would settle for a well-placed bullet. He just didn't want any of them to die quickly. He wanted them to think about their miserable lives for a while before they died.

He wanted them to taste his hatred on their lips before they bled out and left this mortal coil. He wanted them to know that their criminal acts called for severe consequences. He wanted them to know that he was the death they had feared all their lives.

Finally, Joby let his thoughts and his hatred die down and he lay in a huddle, closing his eyes and shutting out the images, the horrible images of his wife at the hands of Popper and his bunch. Instead, he thought of her hair on their pillow at home, spread out like a fan, the low lamplight making her tresses gleam like sunlight on a crow's wing.

And in the rain he smelled the earthy perfume of her, the musk of her womanhood. In the flashes of lightning, he thought he saw her standing in the gossamer veils of rain beckoning to him.

And in between claps of thunder, he could hear McKinney sobbing like a man in a cell who had been sentenced to death and was just waiting for the executioner to come and put the knotted rope around his neck and pull the lever on the trapdoor that would drop him into eternity, blotting out all pain, all memory.

29

THE BRUNT OF THE THUNDERSTORM PASSED SHORTLY BEFORE dawn. There were still intermittent wind gusts and spatters of rain, but Joby knew that the worst was over. He was glad he had put up the shelters on high ground so that most of the water had drained away during the heaviest rains.

He crawled out of his small lean-to and walked over to check on the horses. He grained each one, including McKinney's, using his hat for a feeder. The horses, he knew, would need all the strength they could muster for the long ride ahead.

He did not want ZP and his men to get too far ahead. In his mind, he was already formulating a plan to catch up with him and begin to pare down his numbers. It would take persistence and cunning and he must count on Dolores, his sons and McKinney to follow his orders.

He had not slept much, and he was tired, but he was also strangely exhilarated. He always felt good after a rain, and he knew that sometime that day they would ride into sunlight and dry their bedrolls and themselves. He built a smoke and was shivering in the cold of the predawn darkness, but the bite of the tobacco made him forget the chill and served to calm his mind and allow him to think through his strategy. He had been this way before and he knew something of the habits of the men he was pursuing. ZP was an early riser, just as he was, but the others tended to dawdle and stave off full wakefulness for as long as ZP would allow them to sleep.

By now, Joby figured, the others in the bunch, if not ZP himself, were beginning to relax. If they had a destination in mind, they were looking forward to holing up for a few days and spending some of the money they stole from the Gilmet bank. Even ZP was prone to enjoying the spoils of his victories. And, too, Joby knew they would have to resupply, get food not only for themselves but for their horses. He expected that Popper would soon begin to leave horses behind, ones he no longer needed, the ones that were slowing him down. He had killed one, but he still had a remuda left that was hindering him, slowing him down, eating up his limited resources of feed and water.

Joby finished his smoke and patted the horses in reassurance. A light rain fell in a steady mist, and he knew it was time to wake the others and start the day early, before the sun was up.

Joby shook the boys awake first. They were as wet as he was and seemed glad to get up and move around.

"Saddle up," Joby told them and then woke up Dolores, held her until she stopped shivering and then shook McKinney by the shoulders. The man came awake right away, but it was obvious that he had had a hard night. He rubbed his eyes and stood in the darkness as if trying to remember where he was.

"Early," McKinney said.

"We're going to make a good run at them today."

"You can't track in this wet."

"They'll take the easiest road west. I'll find them sooner or later."

"Later is what I'm afraid of," McKinney said.

"You have too many fears for a growed man, McKinney."

"I'll get my horse," McKinney grumbled and stumbled away, as soggy as the rest of them. They rode through the dripping trees back to the muddy road.

Joby drove them all hard through veils of mist and occasional squalls of wind and rain. They ate in their saddles, chewing on jerky and hardtack, washing the food down with water from their canteens. The road was muddy and, in low places, filled with standing water. The creeks were full and running fast. The skies were leaden, but the clouds began to thin after only an hour or two and in the west they could see patches of blue beyond puffs of wispy clouds that seemed to trail lazily behind the wake of the storm that had passed to the east during the night.

As the early morning wore on, they all shed their slickers and let the breezes dry their clothing. To the east, the black clouds began to disappear and the sun finally emerged in a blue sky flocked with patches of delicate white clouds. The sun burned into their backs as the tall pines, too, began to thin out, replaced by huge grassy swales and scattered clumps of hardwoods and brush that offered better views of the vast land ahead of them.

The road began to dry and the puddles shrank. The mud thickened and hardened, and shrank into clumps of wet dirt. The country was sparsely populated and although they saw a few roads leading off from the main one, Joby saw no reason to veer from his course.

"Is that one of the horses you saw in town?" Joby asked McKinney, pointing to a lone sorrel gelding standing hipshot off the road.

"Yep, I think that was one of 'em."

"Good. We'll probably see more."

Then Joby saw something about the horse that made him rein up and come to a halt.

"What's the matter?" McKinney asked.

"That horse yonder. It's standing kinda funny."

"Just hipshot is all."

"I'm going to take a look," Joby said.

He rode toward the horse, the others following him. The horse looked spooked but as it tried to sidle away, it limped. Then it stopped.

Joby cursed under his breath.

"Horse is lame," McKinney said. "That's why they left it here."

"Maybe," Joby said. He rode up to the horse and then climbed out of the saddle. He put his hand on the horse's neck, soothing it, then slowly walked to the rear, running his hand along the horse's back and down it's flank. He squatted and looked at the hoof dangling in the air.

"What is it?" McKinney asked as Joby looked back up at him.

"Take a look if you like. That bastard Popper cut its hamstring. Clean through."

"What?"

Joby leaned over and looked at the other leg, the rear one with the hoof still on the ground. The hoof was barely touching. That hamstring was cut, too, though not so deeply as the other.

"Popper made this horse lame," Joby said. "So's nobody could ride it."

"He'll just suffer and die," Dolores said, a sadness in her voice. "That's so cruel."

"Damned cruel," Joby said, drawing his pistol.

"No, Pa, don't," Mark said, as his father walked to the horse's front. They all heard the click of the hammer as Joby cocked it.

"Leave him be, Mark," Forrest said. "He's goin' to put that poor horse out of its misery."

Joby put the barrel of his pistol up to the ear of the horse and pulled the trigger. There was a loud explosion and the horse dropped as if it had been poleaxed. It landed with a thump, twitched its legs spasmodically, quivered for a few seconds and then lay still.

Dolores gasped. Mark let out a small cry of dismay. Forrest clamped his teeth tightly and a nerve quivered along his jawline. McKinney's face softened to a pale pudding as the blood drained from his cheeks.

Joby ejected the brass shell casing from the cylinder of his revolver and slid another .44/40 round into the empty sleeve.

"Let's go," he said.

Mark looked back at the dead horse as they rode back to the road. He shook his head sadly and then looked at his brother.

"I reckon Pa had to do it," he said.

"That horse was suffering real bad, Mark." Forrest sighed. "Pa didn't want it to suffer no more."

"Yeah, you're right, Forrest."

The five rode for another mile, each silent with thought, as if they had just come from a solemn funeral.

Then, suddenly, faint hoof marks began to appear in the drying road and these became sharper and more pronounced as Joby pressed on, his blood running hot now that he had picked up the track once again.

"Pa, is that them?" Forrest asked, as he rode up alongside his father.

"Yeah. They're damned fresh, too."

"Where they headed?"

"If they keep on this road, they'll likely wind up in Fort Worth. If they take the forks up ahead, they'll be heading for Waco."

"You ever been there?"

"Where?"

"Well, either Fort Worth or that other'n."

"I've been to Waco and Fort Worth. So has Popper. So has his bunch."

"Which way do you figger they'll go?"

"Well, they've gone a long ways between towns and they'll want to light pretty soon. I'd say they might go to Fort Worth first, then head south to Waco."

"Are we going to catch up to them today?"

"Those tracks are less than an hour old," Joby said. "We might. We ought to. Depends on what other tricks ZP has up his damned sleeve."

"Bet you can figger 'em out, though, Pa."

"I hope so." Joby turned in the saddle and looked at McKinney and his sister. "Look, I'm going to ride on ahead. You keep up the same pace you're goin' now. If you hear shootin', you come careful and ready to fight."

McKinney opened his mouth as if to say something, but Joby glared at him and said, "You do what you're told, McKinney, or you won't ride another foot. Clear?"

"Clear," McKinney said, a scowl appearing on his face in an instant.

Joby put the spurs to his horse and rode on ahead of the others. He kept his eyes on the freshening tracks, but he also kept an eye on the road ahead and the surrounding land. He didn't want any surprises. He had a hunch that he would catch up to ZP and his men and maybe work a surprise or two on them.

The road forked and the tracks took to the south, which would take the outlaws away from Fort Worth. Joby now figured that ZP might be headed to his old haunts along the Brazos, maybe head west of Waco. He would just have to ride it out, but he'd had that same thought in the back of his mind ever since he had left home.

The tracks were now very fresh. Some hoofprints still had puddles in them and the mud on the sides had not yet dried in the sun. Joby's blood quickened, and he slipped his rifle from its scabbard and thumbed the hammer back to full cock. He laid the long gun across his pommel at an angle, the stock resting on the inside of his right leg, just below the hip.

Some instinct inside him, something borne of war and fighting, of tracking and hunting, made Joby slow his horse and take it down to a walk. The road took a bend a hundred yards ahead, and he could not see beyond that point. The road curved off to the west and some trees stood between him and the rest of it, not thick, but sparse enough so that he could see anything that might be moving in that direction.

And as Joby drew closer to the bend, he did see something. A horse. No, two horses. And then, as he drew closer, he saw more than two and they were not in the field, but seemed to be either right on the road, or right next to it.

Joby left the road and angled toward the trees, to the left of where he was seeing the horses. As he rode closer, he heard men's voices, voices that were low and gruff, raspy from drink or from staying up late at night. In moments, he was hearing actual words.

"I hate like hell to be a-doin' this," one man said, and Joby recognized the voice.

"Just grab aholt and do your cuttin' quick. We got to get the hell out of here. ZP's wearing out leather."

He recognized the second voice, too, and he was pretty sure what the men were doing.

Frank Duggan and Roy Botts.

Joby saw both men kneeling down behind unsaddled horses, their knives flashing in the weak sunlight. He heard the horses scream then as their tendons were severed and

Roy cursed as he stood up, backing away from the injured horse.

Then Duggan finished his work, the horse shrieking in pain and trying to hop around before its hindquarters sagged and its legs collapsed beneath, folding the animal to the ground, kicking and writhing.

Joby's blood boiled and there was a throbbing at his temple as his pulse pounded. His stomach roiled as it always did at such times—such times when he was just about to take a human life, to kill a man who had lost the right to live.

30

The screaming whinnies of the horses floated like scarlet ribbons on the air as Joby, a fierce light in his eyes, clenched his teeth and rode toward Roy Botts. The horse that was down began to whicker pitifully as it struggled to regain its feet, wallowing in soft mud, trying to rise by using only its forelegs.

Botts, a short-statured man, whip-thin, turned at the sound of approaching hoofbeats, his bearded face masking his fear. He dropped his knife onto the ground and his right hand dove like a hawk's shadow toward his holstered pistol.

Joby emerged from the cover of trees and Botts's eyes widened like tiny, round windows. His hand grasped the butt of his pistol and he yelled, "Look out, Frank," just as Joby swung the barrel of his rifle out and away from the pommel, pointed it straight at Butts and squeezed the trigger.

Duggan, who had been standing behind his own horse, ducked and snapped the straight razor shut before tucking it back into his pocket. He stepped out into the open just in time to see Botts take the bullet square in the gut.

There was a slapping sound that followed the crack of the rifle and Botts bent in half with the force of the blow. Blood spewed from his abdomen and a wad of flesh as big as a pie plate flew from his back in a lush crimson spray of blood that was like a pink cloud of cherry dust. Botts himself flew backward as if struck with a sixteen-pound maul and skidded through the mud on his backside as if jerked by a rope snubbed to a pulley.

Duggan clawed at the butt of his pistol as Joby swerved his horse and headed straight for him, cocking the lever of his Henry with a smooth, methodical motion.

"You bastard," Duggan yelled, his florid face puffed out from exertion as if all the fat from his neck had suddenly risen to his cheeks. His beard did not mask the flush of blood that suffused his features until he looked as if his face had been boiled in a vat of crushed cranberries.

Joby knew he presented a rich target for Duggan. He turned his horse sideways, swung out of the saddle on the side farthest away from Duggan, then walked with the horse a few yards until he had a clear view of Duggan.

Duggan started firing his pistol, but he seemed unable to find his target. Joby walked toward him, holding his rifle level just below his hip until he was within forty yards. Then he squeezed the trigger, aiming by an instinct honed from years of hunting game and from his time in the Second Texas during the war.

The bullet smashed into Duggan's right shoulder, knocking the pistol from his hand and spinning him around with the force of the bullet.

Duggan screamed in pain and tried to keep his balance, tripping and stumbling away from Joby. Joby levered another cartridge into the chamber and put his rifle to his shoulder. He took dead aim on Duggan's left leg, right at the knee. He squeezed the trigger and saw dust fly off the back of Duggan's pants as the bullet entered behind the knee and shattered it like a clay bowl. Duggan's leg crumpled and went out from under him. He toppled over, screaming in pain. Blood poured from his leg and began to pool up in the mud.

Duggan reached out for his pistol. Then he looked up as a shadow fell across him.

Joby looked down at Duggan, then worked the lever of his rifle, jacking another shell into the firing chamber. He put the muzzle of the rifle square against Duggan's forehead, right between his eyes.

"You haven't got long, Frank. My finger's slick with sweat and is liable to squeeze of its own accord."

"So what, Joby? You go right ahead, you bastard."

"How much pain can you stand, Frank? Not much, as I remember. Back in Corinth you got a splinter of lead in your arm and bawled like a baby with the colic."

Duggan's face reddened even more. He doubled up his nearly severed leg and rocked back and forth as he tried to level out the pain that was sending red hot splinters of iron through his brain.

"You . . . you . . ." Duggan spluttered. Then his gaze shifted from Joby's face to a point behind where Joby Redmond stood.

"I hear 'em," Joby said. He did not look around.

"You call that a damned posse?" Duggan asked.

"I call it family, Frank."

Duggan spat and cringed as Joby tapped his broken knee with the toe of his boot. A few yards away, Roy Botts groaned, his body splayed in the muddy road like a man crucified without the benefit of a wooden cross.

"You gutted him, Redmond. For God's sake, put him out of his misery. Ain't you got no heart at all?"

McKinney, Dolores and Joby's sons rode up alongside and looked down at Joby and Duggan. McKinney had an odd look on his face, as if he were in shock and could not believe his eyes.

"That's one of 'em, Redmond. What're you waitin' for? Put a damned bullet in his heart."

"Hold on, Mac," Joby said. "Look yonder, beyond those three horses they've already ruined. What do you see?"

McKinney and the others looked down the road a few yards. He shook his head. Dolores's mouth fell open. The boys looked bewildered.

"Did you get 'em all?" McKinney asked.

"I noticed that some of the horse tracks weren't very deep," Joby said. "So I knew some of the horses had lost their riders."

"I don't get it, Redmond."

"One of ZP's tricks. He left these two to ride on with the string, then cripple 'em. Duggan here and Botts over there just didn't get it done in time."

"You mean ZP and my daughter aren't here?"

"That's right, McKinney. ZP must have had some horses stashed. He used the rainstorm to get away, leaving no tracks. He took his saddles and gear with him. I figure he and Hayes and Richardson are long gone from these parts."

Joby looked at Duggan, who had a trace of a smirk on his face.

"Did I get it right, Frank?"

"I ain't sayin'," Duggan said.

Joby touched a toe to Duggan's shattered knee. Duggan screamed in pain and doubled over. There was no place on his leg he could touch to take away that fire that went clear through his body and his brain.

"You want this to quit, Frank, you just speak right up. I want to know where ZP is headed."

Duggan moaned and glared at Joby in defiance.

Joby touched the smashed knee with the barrel of his rifle. Duggan squirmed and tears streamed from his closed eyes as he tried his best not to scream.

"I can do this all day, Frank."

"Damn you, Joby Redmond. You know I can't stand pain like this."

"Maybe Roy can take it a little better. He's still alive, you know. And one of you is damned sure going to talk."

Dolores turned away as her brother stepped down on Duggan's knee, crushing it into the ground. This time, Duggan screamed like a woman, long and loud and high-pitched. Still, Joby did not take his foot from the knee. Duggan squirmed and tried to crawl away, but he was pinned to the ground like a bug with a needle through its gut.

"All right, all right, stop," Duggan screeched. "I can't take no more."

"Talk fast, or I might shoot a hole through that other knee and a few more places. Give you some wounds that may not kill you, but will damned sure make you wish you were dead ten times over, Frank."

Duggan winced. His face turned red, then drained of all color. Sweat oiled his features and body until he was reeking with the smell of it.

"You know ZP's got him a place up on the Brazos, west of Waco. He had it before the war."

"I heard that," Joby said.

"He's headed there, with the women. Me'n Roy are supposed to meet him there. We was left behind to slow you down, keep you guessin'."

"Where did he get horses?"

"We left a string with a friend back up north a ways, not far from where we cut that other horse. ZP just walked over and saddled up last night."

"How far from Waco is ZP's hideout?" Joby asked.

"Ain't far, but it's hard to find. It ain't right on the river. Maybe twenty mile. Been a long time since I been there."

"You've got to do better than that, Frank." Joby stepped close and lifted his left foot just above Duggan's crushed kneecap.

Duggan's face paled once again.

Dolores turned away. Mark and Forrest watched their father in fascination, but there was fear on their faces, too, as if they were watching another man, a man they did not know, standing there in their father's body.

"Big sand dunes," Duggan said quickly. "'Tween the river and the hideout. Lots of sand, like a damned desert and at the river, three white oaks set close together. You . . . well, you turn south at them trees and start climbing those big old dunes. About two, three miles is where he has his hideout. From there he can see anybody comin' for a long ways in ever' direction."

"You'd better be tellin' it straight, Frank. I got another .44 cartridge I'm just itchin' to use on you."

"Hell, I'd pay you to shoot me if you'd put a ball in my brain. I can't stand no more of this. I won't never be able to walk again."

"No, likely you won't."

Joby turned away from Duggan and walked over to Botts. Botts had lost a lot of blood, but he was still alive. Just barely.

McKinney rode over, too. Dolores led the boys away as if to shield them from seeing any more brutality. Joby could hear them murmuring something to Dolores, could hear her voice, low and soothing, as if she were their mother. Joby felt a pang of sadness as he thought about Felicia.

"Roy," Joby said, "I meant for you and Duggan to die real slow. How's it goin'?"

"Bastard," Botts breathed in raspy tones. "Prime bastard."

"I don't take no enjoyment from this, Roy, but you and ZP done a lot of harm and you killed my ma and stole my woman."

"And my daughter," McKinney said.

"Shut up, McKinney," Joby said.

"You . . ." Botts said, speaking slowly and in a barely audible voice, ". . . you ain't got your woman no more, Joby. And, that man's daughter . . . she's just meat for the pokin'. We all had us a turn at her ever' day and ever' night. She was more'n willin', that Ronnie gal. And your Felicia, she's real experienced like them honky-tonk gals in Fort Worth."

McKinney boiled over. He jerked his rifle from its scabbard. Froth streamed from the corners of his mouth and he lifted the rifle to cock it.

Joby whirled on him.

"McKinney, if you use that rifle, I'll blow you right out of the saddle."

"How dare you listen to that man and let him live," McKinney spat. "What he's done to my daughter and to your wife. . . . Ye gods, the man's a savage."

"He's a dying savage, McKinney. And that's the way it's going to be. Now get on out of here. We've got a lot of hard riding to do."

"I want to kill him. I want to kill both of them," McKinney said, his face contorted in rage.

"They're already dead," Joby said. "Let them watch the buzzards circle for a while and think about those big beaks and those big claws tearing out their innards while there's still breath in them."

Joby reached down and lifted Botts's pistol from its holster. He tucked it inside his belt.

"Just so you won't be tempted to throw down on yourself, Roy. I expect by early afternoon you'll see those buzzards comin' for you."

Then Joby walked away. McKinney glared at Botts, then reluctantly sheathed his rifle. He followed Joby back to his horse, still livid with rage.

"He might not die," McKinney said. "And he ought to. Now, when we've got him on the ground."

"You kill him, then, McKinney. Just shoot his brains out and deliver him from pain and remorse and guilt for what he's done. Just go ahead. Shoot both of these animals and then live with yourself. Mercy is a good thing, sometimes, but think about the mercy they showed your daughter while you're pulling the trigger."

Joby climbed onto his horse and rode over to Duggan. He still had his rifle in his hands.

"You just goin' to leave us like this, Joby?" Duggan asked, a pleading in his voice.

"No, I reckon not, Frank. You still got too much kick left in you."

Then Joby took dead aim on Duggan's other leg and fired straight at the kneecap. The heavy slug tore through meat and bone and gristle and ripped out veins and splintered most of what held the knee together. Duggan screamed until he was hoarse and rolled around as if trying to escape from the pain from which there was no escape.

McKinney looked at Joby and swallowed air as if to get a bad taste out of his mouth.

"Redmond. Jesus the Christ."

And that was all that McKinney could say, for there were no words to express his tangled feelings, the shock that had jolted him from his world into one he knew he would never understand.

31

Joby saw that McKinney wasn't going to let it drop. Even as he stepped up the pace and rode west at a mile-eating clip, the distraught father was persistent.

"I still don't understand why you didn't kill those two men back there, Redmond. You shot those wounded horses easily enough. If you didn't have the stomach for it, you should have let me kill those outlaws."

"I wanted them to suffer. Make up some for the suffering they caused. It was a hell of a lot harder to kill those poor, innocent horses."

"But, they'll recover and do it again."

"They won't."

"They won't do it again, or they won't recover?"

"Roy Botts was gutshot. He's got a hole in his back big enough to drive a wagon through. Frank Duggan is leaking blood like a sieve from that second shot. My bullet cut through a big old artery."

"You can't be sure of that."

"I'm sure. I saw enough wounds in the war so that I

know when a man is dying or not. Those two are probably already dead."

"Still, I wish I could have seen them die. Just to make sure. Those two sure as hell sullied my daughter. And your wife, Redmond. How can you let animals like that live? Even for a little while, when you've got them dead in your sights."

"McKinney, you're eatin' yourself alive with that kind of talk. You can't change what's been done, no more than I or anybody else can."

"I want justice."

"The Mexes have a sayin' about that, McKinney. *No hay justicia en el mundo.*"

"What in hell does that mean?"

"It translates: 'There's no justice in the world,' but it means a hell of a lot more."

"I don't foller you, Redmond."

"It means you're not liable to find much justice in this world, but there's a price to pay in the next life. The Mexes take great store in justice and in things like heaven and hell."

"Do you?"

"There's some truth to what they say."

"So, you think those two will pay later on, after they die?"

"I don't think about it, McKinney. And neither should you. I hated those men. I hated what they've done. But I gave them what I thought they deserved and it had nothing to do with justice."

"You've got a strange mind, Joby Redmond. It's kinda twisted up."

Joby chuckled. "Maybe so," he said. "But it's all I've got to go on."

"Well, you should have killed those two. Or let me kill them."

"You can kill the next one, McKinney."

"Is that a promise, Redmond?"

"The next one won't be lyin' down all shot up. He'll be standin' there with a gun in his hand looking you right square in the eyes. You'll probably be shakin' like a dog, shittin' peach seeds and soilin' your damned britches."

McKinney cursed, but didn't say anything.

Joby kicked his horse and rode on ahead just to get away from McKinney and his constant talk.

Sometime later, Mark and Forrest galloped up behind him, and by then Joby was glad for some company.

"Pa," Mark said, right off, "how come you didn't kill those two bad men?"

Joby smiled. Mark was the one who could never keep anything on his chest. He always got it off right away.

"I did kill them."

"You did?" Forrest asked.

"I just killed them a little slower than Bill McKinney wanted me to."

Both boys laughed, but their laughs were nervous, tentative. Joby knew they had other things on their mind. But McKinney had a mouth that spewed poison. Especially to young lads not yet used to the ways of the world.

"Auntie Dolores told Mr. McKinney that you knew what you were doing. She said you were a brave and fair man."

"That was nice of her," Joby said. "Anything to shut McKinney up, I reckon."

"You've killed men before, I reckon," Mark said.

"Why do you say that, Mark?"

"'Cause we figgered you had. When you was in the war."

"I suppose so, then. That's what war is all about. Killing other men."

"Why?" Forrest asked. He was the reflective one, questioning everything, studying, thinking.

"Good question, Forrest. Not easily answered."

"But you can answer it, Pa," Mark said. "Right?"

"Partly, maybe. Man is an animal. All animals kill for food. Everything in this world eats everything else. Man is the only one who kills for sport and I guess war is a sport for some men. And I guess some men, they call them cannibals, do eat the men they kill. But mostly, men fight each other and when they want something real bad, they're willing to kill for it."

"I can't imagine killing anybody," Forrest said.

"I can," Mark said. "If they were trying to kill me. Or hurt somebody I really cared a lot about, like Pa or Ma, or you, Forrest."

"Some men don't want to kill, but sometimes they don't have a choice," Joby said. "I don't like to shoot dogs, either. But if one goes mad and starts biting people, I sure as hell am goin' to shoot it plumb dead."

"Like those men," Mark said.

"Yeah," Joby said.

"I'm glad you didn't kill them, Pa," Forrest said. "It don't seem right to me."

"Oh, they're probably dead by now, Forrest. I killed them all right."

"Why didn't you just kill them dead, Pa?" Mark asked.

"I wanted to," Joby said. "But, I also wanted them to suffer some for what they did to your grandma and those other people back in Gilmet. I wanted them to think about where they were going when they bled out. I wanted them to think about hellfire."

Both boys let out long, breathy sighs as if the darkest secrets of the world had suddenly been revealed to them. They did not speak for a while, and Joby knew they were wrestling with consciences not yet fully formed. They were preoccupied with those two men the same as McKinney was, but not for the same reasons. Now, he thought, they were probably thinking of their grandmother and those dead people back in town. And a lot of other things besides, like hellfire and damnation.

"I don't see any tracks," Mark said, after a while. "Where are we going?"

"I figure ZP and the other two men with him, Pete Hayes and Richard Lee, are going to cut into this road pretty soon. I feel pretty sure they're heading for Waco."

"Where's Waco?" Forrest asked.

"South and west. A long ride."

"More than a hundred miles?" Mark asked.

"I reckon. We'll pick up their tracks pretty soon, I'm thinkin'."

"How do you figger all this out?" Forrest wanted to know.

"Auntie Do says he was a scout for the Confederate Army," Mark said, puffing up with his knowledge.

"You hunted them down?" Forrest asked.

"I hunted these men down once. Now, no more questions. You better slow up and wait for your Aunt Do. She can probably use some company. McKinney can wear a person out real quick."

"All right, Pa," Forrest said. "We thought you might be gettin' lonesome up here."

"Yeah. We was lonesome back with McKinney," Mark said. "He sure does talk a lot about his daughter. It made me a little sick."

Joby chuckled. He waved to the boys and spurred his horse. If he figured right, they should be cutting the trail of ZP and his two henchmen pretty soon. The road was drying out fast, but he knew he would be able to read signs.

He just didn't know how much of a jump ZP had on him. But if ZP had ridden through the night he could be some distance away. And he would be getting tired about now and looking for a place to hole up.

But then, ZP didn't always do what a man expected him to do.

He was like an animal, more than most men, and he had all the cunning and treachery of a predator, a wolf or a lion, and he would kill, whether cornered or not.

Joby ate in the saddle, and by late afternoon he found a road cutting into the one he was on. There were five sets of horse tracks. He studied them for a long time so that he would later recognize them wherever he found them.

The tracks, however, were a good six or seven hours old. And from the looks of the tracks, the horses ZP had gotten were big and strong and showed no signs of weariness.

Joby shook off his own tiredness and looked at the sun as it rode slowly down the western sky. He might be able to go on, but he knew his sister and his sons would need rest soon.

He didn't give a damn about McKinney, and wished he would just lie down and sleep into next week and never open his mouth again about his sullied daughter, Veronica.

32

JOBY KEPT UP THE PACE THROUGH SMALL SETTLEMENTS, PAST isolated farmhouses where he was able to restock by buying food and staples from farmers who welcomed company, any company. At night, Dolores played the dulcimer after supper, and Joby saw to it that they all turned in early, with none of them on watch.

The tracks grew fresher every day, and just before they reached the outskirts of Waco, he noticed that one of the horses ridden by the outlaws had gone lame. As they rode into black prairie country and struck the Brazos, Joby knew they were getting close. ZP and his bunch could not have gotten there more than an hour before them. And he'd have to replace that lame horse. Another of the horses had thrown a shoe and he knew that one of the men would have to stop at a livery or a blacksmith's.

Beyond Waco, he knew, the flat prairie would change to rolling hills and the land would grow more rugged. This was where Americans had settled in the 1840s and had to fight the Tonkawa, Waco and Wichita, all along the Brazos and Bosque rivers.

"We're getting close," Joby told Dolores and the boys. "You can see the buildings yonder, all along the Brazos."

"I see them," Dolores said. "It's nice to see a big town for a change. But it makes me feel dirty."

"Well, you have plenty of river to bathe in."

"I'd like to put up at a hotel," she said.

"Me, too," the boys chorused.

Joby smiled wanly. He supposed he could leave his family there and go on alone. He'd have McKinney tagging along, but he could deal with that. He was pretty sure Bill McKinney would not want to stay in a hotel as long as the outlaws were on the run.

"Joby, do you have enough money to buy us some clothes in town?" Dolores asked. "We're almost in rags. A bath and some fresh clothes would do wonders for our spirits."

"I took all the money I had in the house, Do. There's plenty left to buy clothes. What about the hotel?"

"I'm still thinking about that," she said.

"This road becomes Market Street. There's a livery stable at this end of town, and not far, a block or two maybe, there's a mercantile store. Why don't you take Mark and Forrest down there, get some clothes and wait for me and McKinney."

"You're taking him to the stables, Joby?"

"The man's like my shadow. I can't shake him."

Dolores laughed. Her face had darkened from the sun, and she had acquired a dusky beauty like some of the Mexican women Joby had seen. Her black tresses and white teeth transformed her into an exotic creature, oddly childlike, but truly a woman, full-blown.

"Sometimes, back there, I thought you were going to shoot McKinney out of the saddle."

"It never entered my mind, Do."

She laughed again. He dug into a pocket and took out a

wad of money. He peeled off several bills and handed them to his sister.

"Thanks," she said.

"Don't take too long getting those clothes. We're right behind ZP. If he stopped to shoe a horse, I'll get him."

"Maybe we ought to be with you when you go to the livery."

"No. I want to see if McKinney has the backbone to shoot a man who's looking straight at him."

"What if he doesn't?"

"Then he's just one worry. I can handle that. You and the boys wait for me, or us, at the mercantile, Do. You can bathe once we get out of town."

"Maybe we won't have to leave town."

"You mean . . ."

"I mean you may get 'em all right here," she said. "Get Felicia and Ronnie back."

"I've been disappointed before," he said.

And then they reached the town. Joby told McKinney what Dolores and his boys were going to do and what he expected to find at the livery.

"You think all of 'em will be there?" McKinney asked. "Maybe you ought to keep the boys with us."

"They might get in the way. You ready to shoot a man?"

"I'm ready," McKinney said.

But Joby wondered. He thought he detected a tremor of fear in McKinney's voice.

Joby reined his horse to a stop and turned, waiting for Dolores and the boys to catch up to him. McKinney halted his horse, too, a quizzical look on his tanned face.

"Do, there's the livery up ahead. You and the boys just ride on by. Don't look in that direction. The mercantile's not far, on the left side, if I remember right."

"Have you been there before, Joby?"

"Yeah. Long time back."

"All right."

Joby watched them go and still he waited.

"What are we going to do?" McKinney asked.

"We're going to hitch our horses this side of the livery and walk in there with just our sidearms."

"Shouldn't we take the rifles and be ready?"

"You can advertise you're a manhunter if you want to, Mac. My idea is just to slip in the back and see what we see."

"Just you and me, eh?"

"Just you and me," Joby said.

Joby and McKinney rode on and then Joby turned his horse at a tack store near the stables, a small wooden building that had been weathered gray by wind and rain for some thirty years. The windows were dusty, but he could see saddles and bridles through the glass, the gleam of bits and spurs and D rings struck by the slanting sun. He slid down from the saddle and wrapped his reins around the top rail. McKinney did the same. Joby headed for a narrow space between the little store and the livery stables. The sign over the livery read: J. STEVENS, PROP. It, too, was weathered and faded, but was pretty much as he remembered it.

A breeze railed down the dirt street, blowing dust and scraps of paper and old leaves before it as Joby and McKinney stepped between the two buildings. It was quiet and dark there in the narrow passageway to the back alley. When they emerged, they saw the corrals on the other side of the alley. There were tanks inside the corrals and rusted pumps outside, their spouts turned toward the stock tanks. Horses stood and switched their tails, eyeing the two men as they stepped back out into the sunlight, their clothes whipping in the brisk breeze.

"You stay right behind me. Let your eyes adjust to the dim light when we get inside," Joby said.

McKinney nodded.

The back doors were open slightly. Joby was careful to make no noise when he walked up to them. It was darker inside than outside and he stood at the opening for a few moments and looked inside. He heard a man grunting and breathing, the harder breath of a horse, louder than the man's. Then Joby heard the ring of a hammer on iron and the clink of a horseshoe on the heavy plane of an anvil. He smiled and stepped quickly between the doors and stood inside. McKinney followed him.

Richard Lee Richardson stood over the anvil, a horseshoe in one hand, a hammer in the other. Another man stood by the bellows over the coals of a hot fire. Dust motes floated in the air, lit by the shafts of sunlight that streamed through the cracks in the old building.

"Johnny Stevens," Joby said. "Step away from there and keep your hands in sight."

"That you, Joby Redmond?" Stevens said. "Been a mighty long . . ."

Joby drew his pistol. Stevens, his hair graying at the temples, his clean-shaven face glistening with a sheen of sweat, backed away from the bellows, his hands rising to a point about six inches above his lean shoulders.

Richard Lee stood there, gape-mouthed, his light shirt stained with perspiration and clinging to his torso like wet canvas. He was taller than Stevens, and ten years older. His face was lined with furrows and looked like old, tanned leather. His pistol jutted from the holster on his hip, within easy reach.

Joby looked around the stables quickly. There were two other horses in stalls and the one that Richardson was shoeing.

"You all that's here, Johnny?" Joby asked.

"Yep, Popper left a good ten, fifteen minutes ago. With fresh horses. Paid me cash."

"You just lean against a post, Johnny, and stay out of this. Close your eyes if you want to."

"I'm fine," Stevens said. He backed up to one of the stalls and stood there staring at McKinney and Joby.

"Can we talk about this, Joby?" Richardson asked.

"Looks like you got left behind, Richard Lee."

"Well, ZP was in a temper."

"I hope he paid you off. He didn't leave a cent with Frank or Roy."

"You rub them out, Joby? ZP figgered you might. Who you got with you?"

Joby could hear the clack of McKinney's tongue licking his dry lips.

"Frank and Roy are meat for the buzzards and worms. My wife all right? This man's daughter?"

"Oh, that's who he is. Why, shore, Joby. The gals is just fine, perky as meat-fed pups."

"You bastard," McKinney breathed.

"Go ahead, Mac," Joby said. "You wanted to kill one of the outlaws. This is your chance."

Joby saw the flicker in Richardson's eyes. He stepped away from McKinney, quiet as a shadow.

Out of the corner of his eye he saw McKinney's hand move toward his pistol. But Joby knew he would be too slow. At that same instant, Richardson went into a lunging crouch and threw the hammer straight at McKinney. Then his hand streaked toward his pistol while he hurled the horseshoe at Joby with his other hand.

Time seemed to stand still for a split-second that seemed like an eternity. McKinney dodged the hammer and clawed desperately for his pistol. He was off balance and taken totally by surprise.

Then time resumed its motion and everything seemed to be happening at once. Stevens dropped into a squat and held his hands over his head as if he were being rained on by fire and hot metal.

Joby felt the horseshoe slam into his shin even as his pistol cleared leather and bucked in his hand with a deafening explosion of powder and flame.

White smoke billowed from the barrel of his pistol and then he heard two more explosions, so close together they sounded like one and the smoke was like a cloud enveloping them all in a gauzy puff of cloth that blotted out every man inside the livery.

A man groaned in pain.

The horses whinnied in terror.

And then, for a moment, there was a silence deeper than night, deeper than the black pit leading straight down into hell.

33

JOBY STRODE THROUGH THE SMOKE, LEAVING TANGLED WISPS in his wake that floated in the beams of sunlight like the remains of ghostly apparitions. He looked down at Richard Lee, his pistol cocked and aimed directly at the wounded man's forehead, not three feet away from the muzzle.

"Something happens when you get hit with a .44 slug, Richard Lee, don't it? It's like gettin' smashed with a twenty-pound maul in the gut. At first you don't feel no pain. You're too busy tryin' to get your breath and clear your mind. Then you can smell your intestines and see them pokin' through your belly like a mess of blue snakes. And your back feels cold air rushing in through a big old hole that feels like it's on fire and you know you're leakin' blood through that hole 'cause you can feel it down your back and seepin' into your britches where you sit down. That what it feels like, you sonofabitch?"

Richard Lee, a bullet hole in his abdomen, looked up at Joby with glazed eyes that flickered with smoke and pale sunlight, glassy eyes that reflected the shock of the bullet's energy that had coursed through him moments before.

"Finish it, Joby," Richardson muttered. "Make it quick, you bastard."

"Was it worth it, Richard Lee? I mean you don't have the money and you'll never see a pretty woman again, let alone put your filthy worm inside one."

Joby heard a rustle of footsteps shuffling through the straw on the dirt floor of the stables. He didn't look up, but he knew McKinney had appeared beside him, and out of the corner of his eye, he saw a thin wisp of smoke curling up from the barrel of Bill's pistol.

"Kill him, Redmond," McKinney growled, a husk in his voice that was like dried oak leaves sliding down a tin roof.

"Go out front, Mac," Joby said. "Wait for me."

"I want to see him die."

"You see him. He's dyin'. Now get out before I lose what temper I got left."

Joby looked at McKinney then, and his eyes burned like hot coals, and McKinney shrank away from that withering look and growled deep in his throat. But he walked away, his pistol dangling at the end of his arm like a useless weight, like some enigmatic piece of iron that had no heart and no soul.

"Johnny," Joby said, when McKinney had left the stable, "keep this to yourself for a while, will you? I need to get after those men that were with this piece of shit. Popper's got my wife and McKinney's daughter with him."

"Whatever you say, Joby. Sure." Stevens got up slowly and walked over to look at the sprawled, angular figure of Richard Lee lying in a pool of blood that widened slowly under his back and rump. "God, I didn't know a bullet could do that much damage to a man."

Richardson's eyes fluttered and his breathing became hard. And every breath brought pain shooting through him as if he were roasting on a spit over a blazing fire.

"Joby, don't leave me like this, huh, will you? Least give me back my own gun so's I can . . ."

"You got a few minutes, Richard Lee, to think about what you done. A little time, maybe, to think about where you're goin', straight to hell."

Richardson opened his mouth as if to say something, but nothing came out except for a wistful gasp that was the last of the air he would ever breathe. His throat rattled with a gurgling sound as his eyes frosted over with the opaque sugar coating of death. He shuddered and his eyes closed in a final seizure. The stink of him rose up as his sphincter muscle collapsed and his dead body voided. Stevens pinched his nose and turned away, his face wrinkled in disgust.

"Give me a couple of hours, Johnny," Joby said. "Then you can call a constable."

"Yeah, Joby. I'll say it was self defense. Which is what it was. Boy, you really hated this man, I reckon."

Joby said nothing. He opened the cylinder gate of his pistol and pushed the ramrod to eject the spent shell. Then he took a bullet from his cartridge belt and slid it into the empty chamber. He eased the hammer down after moving the cylinder slightly so that the hammer rested on the space between two cartridges.

He walked out into the sunlight and saw McKinney standing by his horse next door in front of the tack shop. There was vomit in the street and McKinney's face was sallow, his eyes watery.

"Is he dead?" McKinney asked, in a voice wheezy from the residue of vomit in his throat.

"As a doornail, Mac."

In moments, they were riding down the street, ignoring the passersby who stared at them, the Mexican with his *carreta* stacked high with cut firewood, tapping the rump of his mule with a long stick to keep the animal moving.

The breeze stiffened and dust stung the two men's eyes as they rode toward the mercantile store. Dust began to seep into their sweat-stained clothes and the horses snorted to clear their rubbery noses.

The sign above the store read: WILHITE'S MERCANTILE, G.L. WILHITE, PROP. Next to it was a small building with the legend Mother Mima's Kitchen emblazoned on the windows. Dolores's and the boys' horses were tied to hitch rings outside the café.

As Joby and McKinney rode up to the store, Forrest came out of Mother Mima's, waving. He was wearing a clean, new chambray shirt.

"You want some coffee, Pa?"

"No. Get your auntie and Mark. We haven't got much time."

"Be right back," Forrest said and went back inside the little café.

Joby sniffed the smells coming from Mother Mima's and his stomach roiled with hunger, but he kept looking down Market Street at all the detritus blowing in the wind. He looked up at the sky, at the sun, and figured it was about ten o'clock.

"Those west Texas winds start blowing about this time," he said to McKinney. "It's going to be hard tracking and ZP has fresh horses."

"Maybe we ought to lay up for a day," McKinney said.

"You can lay up here long as you want, Mac. We're close, damned close, and I want my wife back."

"Yeah, you're right. I'm just plumb tuckered is all. I wasn't thinking of poor Ronnie."

"The only good thing about it is that the wind will slow ZP down same as us. As long as we follow the Brazos we're not likely to lose them. If they're going to ZP's hideout."

"Ever been that way before, Redmond?"

"No. Never been past Waco, but I know these winds. Look at some of the stores across the street. People are getting ready for this one."

McKinney followed Joby's gaze. Shopkeepers were hanging blankets on nails and pegs in front of their doors and windows. The blankets were dripping wet.

"To keep the dust out," Joby said.

McKinney bent his head as a gust of wind flung stinging sand into his face and eyes.

Moments later, Dolores, Mark and Forrest emerged from the café. They were carrying sacks full of clothes and food. They all leaned against the wind.

"Got us some hot pork and biscuits," Dolores said. "Bought you some pants and a shirt, too, Joby."

"Get mounted, Do. We're less than an hour from catching up with Felicia."

"In this wind?"

"You can stay in town if you want, Do."

Her jaw hardened and her eyes narrowed.

"We're coming with you," she said.

Joby waited impatiently while the boys and his sister packed the goods onto their horses. Do held on to the sack of hot food as she climbed into the saddle.

"It might get a little sandy when you eat it," she said to Joby. "But it'll put meat on your bones."

"You going to take a bath?" he asked.

"Not today," she said and bent her head against the brunt of the wind.

In a few minutes they were clear of Waco and headed for the sand dunes west of town. Already the tracks of those who had gone before them had faded, and when Joby looked down, all he saw were streamers of sand blowing the road smooth as the bottom of a cast-iron skillet.

The wind was not yet fierce enough to slow them down

much, but Joby could feel it building. He urged his horse onward at a brisk pace, and, to his surprise, he began seeing hoofprints that had escaped the sweep of the winds.

He put spurs to his horse and rode on, his head bent so that the brim of his hat rebuffed most of the blowing sand. He turned back and saw the others trying to keep up. He waved them on, then put his horse to a gallop.

Ahead, he saw the horses, four of them, dim small shapes on the horizon, their bodies broken up by distance and thermal updrafts so that they appeared as dancing ghosts, as figures that appeared whole for one minute and fractured images the next.

He could not make out the riders, but he felt sure he was looking at ZP and Hayes, along with his wife and Veronica.

Then the wind gusted and held steady at what seemed to Joby like forty miles an hour, gusting to fifty or more, and he lost sight of the riders. Joby slowed his horse, saving him for another time when he sighted his quarry. The wind was just too stiff, and he knew it would get worse before this day was done.

"What do you see?" McKinney asked, shouting above the roar of the gale.

"Nothing," Joby said.

"Why were you riding so fast?"

"I'm in a hurry."

"You're crazy, Redmond."

Joby said nothing, but he could almost smell ZP as he watched the tops of sandy mounds blow off like spray from white-capped waves, and the wind swirled and tore at his clothes and ripped his face with sandy claws. He pulled his bandanna up over his nose and mouth, turned and motioned to the others that they should do the same.

His mouth was full of grit and his eyes stung and watered as if they had been pierced by a thousand tiny needles.

The sun grew dim as the dust clouds rose higher and

there seemed to be nothing in front of Joby but desolation and an emptiness that was echoed in his aching heart as he thought about Felicia and the men who held her prisoner in a hell made out of sand and wind.

34

Almost an hour later, the Brazos and all the land around it, including the road, disappeared. The sun vanished as if it had been sucked up in a vortex created by the raging wind. All landmarks vanished in a twinkling as the wind roared across the bleak sands, lifting sheets of it and hurling them like knives or guillotines through the air.

Joby stopped and looked behind him into a sandy nothingness. He struggled to breathe through the dust-clogged bandanna over his face. He ducked his head down and managed to pull air into his lungs, air that tasted like the Sahara or the Gobi, air full of a fine musty dust that might have come from some ancient Egyptian tomb. He blew through his nose and dust spewed out onto his kerchief. His mouth was dry and his teeth covered with grit that made a sawing sound in his brain when he bit down and spat out little chunks of sandy mud.

Where in hell were Dolores and his sons? Where in hell was McKinney, who had been his shadow for hundreds of miles?

Joby felt suddenly engulfed in a great, gray grief, as if

the entire world had disappeared and he was left all alone under a sunless sky, drowning in a vast and unfathomable sea of sand.

"Dolores," Joby yelled and he knew it was a futile cry, for it carried back to him as dead as the air streaming into his tortured lungs.

"Mark! Forrest! McKinney!"

Joby slumped down like a man defeated, praying for mercy, praying for quick dispatch at the hand of his conqueror. A moment later, he straightened up and tried to look around for his bearings. But all he heard was the roaring drone of the wind and the pelt of fine sand against his ears. And, still the wind blew stronger and the land grew darker.

By dead reckoning, Joby retraced his path to the east, toward Waco. It was easier to breathe with the wind at his back, but he was not sure he was headed the right way. He could be making a big mistake trying to find his family and McKinney. Worse, they could be trying to find him, scattering as they wandered in the maelstrom of the sandstorm.

Joby stopped again and listened to the banshee shriek of the wind and felt it ebb against his back. The wailing died away slowly and the wind dropped to a long, moaning sigh and the dust swirling around him seemed to pause and then sink slowly like a billion motes of light being sucked into some black hole of the universe.

Joby saw them, then, all huddled together less than twenty-five yards away. They had their yellow slickers out and were holding them up like tent flaps to ward off the stinging lancets of sand grains pummeling them with relentless fury. Something caught in Joby's throat, a cry of gladness or a sob of joy, and he rode toward them, his heart pounding loudly in his temples, pounding like timpani in a cramped concert hall full of baffles that hung from the ceiling in shrouds of sand.

"You did the right thing," Joby said to McKinney.

"It was your sister's idea. She said you'd find us. I wanted to go on, but she made me stay."

"We thought you was lost," Mark said.

"We'd better turn back, Joby." Dolores dropped her slicker so that he could see her face. "Unless you think it's over with."

"No, this is just a lull. But you should try and get back to town, maybe."

"I can't stand this dust and wind," McKinney said. "I'm plumb beat."

"Mark? Forrest? You want to go back?" Joby let the question hang.

"We don't like it none, either," Forrest said. "But we want to be with you, Pa."

"I'm going on. ZP is running into the same blow as we are. He can't be too far ahead of us."

Joby looked around. He saw the Brazos then, looking almost motionless under the patina of fine sand that lay like dust on a mirror. At least, he thought, he had not lost his sense of direction and that was a comfort to him just then.

"I'm going to go on. I think Popper will head for his hideout, but he may abandon the women along the way."

"You think so?" McKinney asked, an eagerness in his voice that was an unmistakable sign of hope.

"He might."

"Let's go on, then," McKinney said.

"Do?" Joby asked.

"Yes. We'll go on," she said. "We can't just quit now."

"No," Joby said, "we can't. But, let's shake out some rope and run it through our stirrups so that we'll stick together. Mark, your rope."

When they had finished tying the horses together they were all lashed by a gust of wind and then, in the distance, they heard a soft roaring that they knew was the wind returning.

"We've got to find a ford and cross the Brazos," Joby said. "Before the next hard blow. Follow me."

They rode close to the river and suddenly Joby's heart soared when he saw a wide path leading down to it and fresh tracks that had been laid down next to an embankment out of the wind.

He knew that Popper must have crossed there, and when he rode down, trailing the others behind him, he saw the big sand banks that made an eddy in the river and saw the crossing in the shallows before the river rejoined itself.

He urged his horse into the shallow water, touching its flanks to overcome its fear, and they crossed over to the other bank. Joby climbed the embankment and saw the trail, blown free of sand, heading west. Beyond, he saw the cloud of dust coming toward them out of the west, and heard the thin, high shriek of the winds behind it.

Just before the storm closed in again, he saw the three trees that marked the turnoff toward Popper's hideout and, among them, something moved, something small and human, on foot. He turned around to look at McKinney who was just behind him. But McKinney's head was bent down, and so were the heads of the others, so he knew he was the only one who had seen the apparition among the trees.

Joby rode on, toward the three trees, and then, when he reached them, he looked down and saw the pathetic figure of a girl, her hair tangled and thick with sand, her face bruised, welts on her face and neck.

"Veronica?"

McKinney rode up alongside and let out a cry. He jumped from his horse and reached for his daughter. But she turned away from him, sobbing, and McKinney looked up at Joby, bewilderment shadowing his face like some scarlet disease.

They all dismounted and crowded around Veronica McKinney. Her arms bore ugly bruises and her lips were swollen, distorted, the color of crushed blackberries.

Dolores took Veronica in her arms and held her tightly while McKinney stood there, arms dangling helplessly, a scarecrow in the wind and the dust, lost and brainless in the presence of something he could not understand.

"What's wrong with her?" McKinney asked Joby. "She turned away from me."

"She's in shock, Mac. She's just come from another world, you know."

They all stood there as the sand and dust peppered them with stinging nettles that felt like a thousand pinpricks of the flesh and, below the ominous hum of the wind, they could all hear Veronica sobbing, sobbing as if her heart had been torn out of her chest and she was wounded beyond all repair.

35

"YOU POOR THING," DOLORES SOOTHED. "WHATEVER DID those evil men do to you, darlin'?"

"Leave me alone," Veronica spat. She looked like a tigress at bay, Joby thought. "You all don't know nothin'."

"Why are you crying, Ronnie?" Joby asked, giving Dolores a look.

"He—he just left me here. Said—said he didn't want me no more."

"ZP?"

"Yes. I love him," she sobbed.

McKinney reared back as if he had been slapped with a hot stove lid square in the face.

"She—she doesn't know what she's a-sayin'," McKinney spluttered. "Look at her. She's been beaten half to death by that bastard."

"But he kept that bitch, Felicia," Ronnie said. "Oh, I hate her, I hate her."

"Ronnie, stop that kind of talk," McKinney said.

"Shut up, Mac," Joby said, taking his arm and leading him away from his daughter. Dolores began talking to the girl again, in a soft voice that was without accusation. Veronica was talking to her, in low tones that Joby could not hear.

"That's your daughter, Mac. Your own flesh and blood. Quit climbin' her back and let off. She needs your love, not your condemnation."

"All right," McKinney said, but Joby could see that the anger was still seething inside of him. He turned back to Veronica.

"How's Felicia, Ronnie?"

"She's been givin' it to all the men, same as me." Then, with a wicked smile, she said, "and she likes it."

Joby's face darkened, but he said nothing.

"Let's go," he said.

"I threw all their canteens in the river," Ronnie said. "ZP and Pete are thirsty and mad. They'll probably take it out on your precious Felicia now, Mr. Redmond."

Joby wondered why ZP had left Ronnie behind. To slow them down? Because she had gotten too close to him? He kept his thoughts and feelings to himself and mounted up. He sighted from the three trees and headed south by dead reckoning. Ronnie didn't want to ride with her father, so she rode behind Dolores on her horse, the wind blasting them with sand from the northwest now.

The wind subsided some as Mark and Forrest rode up alongside Joby. Forrest pulled his bandanna down from his mouth and spoke first.

"Pa, that girl, that Veronica, she said some terrible things about Ma. About what she did with those men we're after."

"I know."

"Mr. McKinney, he says you don't care about Ma, or anybody else."

"He's wrong, Forrest."

"If Ma did those things that girl said she did," Mark

said, talking through his bandanna, "well, does that mean she doesn't like you anymore?"

"No, Mark. Your mother loves me and you boys."

"Do you still love her after what she did with those men?"

"Your mother's smart, boys. She's doing what she can to survive. She knows those men are animals. She wants to live."

"But, how can you . . . I mean, how can you be with her after . . ." Forrest looked sick to his stomach.

"It's hard to understand, I know. But unless you've been inside the whirlwind of a marriage, you can't really know or understand what it's like between two people who love each other."

"I reckon not, Pa," Mark said. "But that girl, she hates everybody except that Popper. She says she loves him. What happened to her?"

"You think maybe the same thing happened to your mother?" Joby asked. He looked at both boys, then back at the trail ahead. He could see some distance now. The wind was falling off and the sand was drifting away, settling back to the earth.

"I saw some women once who had been rescued from some Comanches," Joby said. "These were white women who were used by the Comanches and who were beaten by them most every day; they were prisoners. Those women said they loved their captors, too, just like Ronnie back there."

"Is Ma going to be like that?" Forrest asked.

"The point is, I've seen the same thing happen to a cur dog. I knew a man who beat an old dog all the time. He kicked it and starved it and cursed it ever since it was a pup. The dog began to think that was the man's way of showing affection. I took that dog away from that man and showed it love. It took some time for it to get used to not being kicked and beat all the time, but finally it knew the difference. And every time it saw a man with a stick, it growled and snarled, and bared its teeth."

"But what if Ma can't get over what happened to her?" Forrest asked.

"Then we have to show her what I showed that dog. That love doesn't mean a beating—ever."

Joby stood up in the stirrups. Ahead, he saw four horses, one of them riderless and the other three ridden by Popper, Hayes and Felicia. Beyond, just poking above the dunes, he saw the top of a cabin.

"There they are, boys, just ahead of us," Joby said. "Come on, we've got to cut them off. We can't let them get to that cabin yonder."

"I see it," Mark said.

"Me, too," Forrest said.

Joby pulled his rifle from his scabbard and told his boys to do the same. He looked back at McKinney and pointed ahead. McKinney nodded and unlimbered his own rifle. Joby gestured for Dolores to hold back. Then he made a circle to McKinney, and pointed to the right.

"Mark, you ride to the right and flank them. Forrest, you come with me. Hurry. Be careful not to shoot your mother, and don't shoot unless you have a clear shot."

They rode fast, flanking the riders ahead. Joby hoped that ZP would not kill Felicia just out of spite. He thought, strongly, that he would use her as a hostage right up to the end.

As Joby drew close on the left flank, Hayes turned around in the saddle, a pistol in his hand. He began to shoot at them. He fired at McKinney and Mark on his right flank. When he ran out of bullets, he holstered his empty pistol and jerked his rifle from its sheath.

Popper spurred his horse and dashed ahead, pulling Felicia and her horse along with him. The riderless horse broke free and trotted away, reins trailing.

Joby rode in close to Hayes and shot his horse in the neck. The horse staggered and went down, throwing Hayes off to its side. Then Joby rode ahead fast and aimed his rifle at the head of Popper's horse. He squeezed the trigger and the bullet smashed into the horse's head. The animal tumbled forward as its forelegs collapsed and ZP flew out of the saddle and skidded through the sand, facedown. Felicia turned her horse quickly, and raced away, toward Joby.

"Go back to where Dolores is," Joby shouted to Felicia. He winced when he saw her battered and bruised face. She nodded grimly and raced on past him, to the rear. He saw the terror in her eyes as she passed and something inside him crumpled and made him sick to his stomach.

Mark rode up to Hayes and dismounted. Then Forrest came to join his brother. Hayes was searching in the sand for his rifle when Joby leaped down on him from his own horse. Hayes rolled away and drew his knife.

Hayes came after Mark while Joby scrambled to get back onto his feet. Then Forrest drew his knife and came toward Hayes. Mark scratched for his own knife, but Hayes lunged and cut Mark on the arm. Hayes turned around and went after Forrest, knife flashing as he closed in for the kill.

Mark hurled himself at Hayes and tackled him. Forrest rushed up then and knocked the knife from Hayes's hand.

"You little bastards," Hayes snarled, "I'll skin you both alive."

Mark and Forrest fell on Hayes as he tried to retrieve his knife and started pummeling him with their fists. Joby saw them and was surprised at their rage. They beat Hayes senseless.

"That's enough, boys," Joby said. "Just keep your guns on him until I get back."

Ronnie jumped from the back of Dolores's horse and came running up. McKinney caught her in his arms.

"Don't kill him," Ronnie screamed. "Please don't kill him."

McKinney balled up a fist and swung his arm. He struck his daughter on the side of the face and knocked her senseless. She fell to her knees. Felicia and Dolores rushed to pick her up and keep her father away from her.

Joby dashed after Popper, who was only a few yards away, dazed and blinded by the sand in his eyes. ZP heard Joby coming and reached for his pistol.

Joby kicked ZP's legs out from under him, then smashed him in the mouth with the butt of his rifle. Popper grunted as blood spurted from his broken nose.

"Joby, you sonofabitch," Popper growled through smashed lips that were bloody and caked with sand.

"You're finished, ZP. Get up."

Joby brought Popper back to where Hayes lay sprawled on his back and threw the man down next to his partner.

Ronnie got up and looked at the two men on the ground. Then, before anyone could react, she snatched her father's pistol from its holster, cocked it and aimed it at Joby.

"You're not going to kill them, Mr. Redmond," Ronnie said. "ZP, I love you," she said, looking at the downed man.

"You bitch," Hayes said.

"Ronnie, give me the gun," Felicia said, holding out her hand. "Don't do anything stupid."

"He's not going to kill my man."

"I'm not going to kill him, Veronica," Joby said. "Give Felicia the gun."

Ronnie hesitated. The pistol wavered back and forth in her hand.

"I'll take it, Ronnie," Felicia said. "Just calm down. You don't want to kill Joby. He's not going to hurt Pete or ZP."

Ronnie sighed and Felicia snatched the pistol from her hand. Everyone let out long sighs.

McKinney took his daughter in his arms and she didn't resist this time. He had tears in his eyes.

Felicia walked over to Hayes, pointing the pistol at him. His eyes widened and Joby saw fear flood them like the shadows cast by birds of prey.

Felicia glared down at both men and started speaking.

"Ronnie," she said, "I want to show you something."

Then Felicia stepped up between Hayes's spread legs and put the toe of her boot on his crotch and pressed down until Hayes screamed.

"Do you think this is what makes a man, Ronnie?" Felicia asked. She pressed down on Hayes's genitals again, harder. Hayes screamed and writhed in pain.

Then she walked over to Popper and nudged him in the crotch.

"Or this?" Felicia asked. Popper gasped. She kicked him in the crotch and he doubled up and wretched.

The boys, Dolores and McKinney, along with Ronnie, all watched Felicia, hypnotized by her.

She walked over to Joby. She put a hand on his chest.

"This is what makes a man, Ronnie," she said. "His heart. Remember that."

Ronnie began sobbing.

"A true man doesn't beat a woman with his fists and boots," Felicia said softly, looking into Joby's eyes with a tenderness that melted something inside him. "A real man doesn't dominate a woman with what is between his legs. These men are beasts, no more than animals. They are not true men, darling Ronnie."

"I—I'm pregnant," Ronnie said.

"I know you are," Felicia said. "And do you know which of the men who stole us is the father?"

Ronnie's eyes flared wildly in their sockets. "N—no," she admitted.

"Neither of these two would be a father to your child, Ronnie. That's why they left you behind. They left you behind so that you and your baby would die."

Ronnie buried her face in her hands and began to sob once more.

Joby put his arm around Felicia and held her close. She winced from the pain where she was bruised.

"Give me back my pistol, Mrs. Redmond," McKinney said, holding out his hand. Felicia gave it to him.

McKinney looked at his daughter, then, as if she were a stranger, someone he had never known.

Then, before anyone could stop him, he walked over to Hayes, aimed his pistol at the man's groin and fired. Hayes jumped and screamed as his crotch boiled out blood. McKinney turned to Popper and shot him in the groin at point-blank range. Popper shrieked in pain and grabbed at his bloody genitals, a look of horror on his face.

Joby snatched the pistol from McKinney.

"Those men were unarmed," Joby said.

"I don't care. They won't never hurt no woman again."

Joby stuffed McKinney's pistol in his belt and said to all of them, "Let's go. Boys, see if you can find that bank money in their saddlebags, then let's head for home."

"What about these men?" Mark asked.

"They'll probably die," Joby said.

"Don't you want to kill them, Pa?" Forrest asked. "For what they did to Ma?"

"No, there's been enough of that. Let nature take its course."

"I want to kill them," McKinney said. "If you'll give me back my pistol."

"You've probably already done that, Mac. But I hope these two bastards live."

"Why?"

"So they'll know they can never be with a woman again. Men, too, will shun them, and that's a punishment worse than death."

The boys dashed off to search the saddlebags on the dead horses for the stolen bank money.

McKinney said nothing for a few moments, then nodded in silent understanding. He looked at his daughter, and took her into his arms once again.

"I'm sorry, Ronnie, for what they did to you," McKinney said.

"You don't know what they did to me, Daddy."

"No, but maybe someday you'll tell me. We can talk about it."

"What about my baby?" Ronnie asked.

"We can adopt it out somewheres."

"No."

"I won't have a little bastard in my home."

"McKinney," Joby said. "Don't blame that baby for what happened to your daughter. It can't choose the way it comes into this world. It can't even choose its father or mother."

"A bastard is a bastard," McKinney said.

The boys returned, carrying four sacks of money. They held them up high and grinned. Then they looked at their father and McKinney and the bags descended to their sides.

"You better think about that, Mac. It's a wise man who knows his own father. I never knew mine."

Mark and Forrest gulped, looked at each other, then back to their father.

"You mean . . ." Forrest began.

"My mother, your grandmother, knew many men, boys.

I was born a bastard, and some would say I remain one to this day."

Joby smiled and looked at Felicia. Dolores smiled, too, for she knew the story. She knew she was really Joby's half-sister. It was a family secret they had held for all these years and she seemed relieved to have it finally let out.

Felicia put her arm around Joby and looked at their sons. She drew herself up proudly and smiled at them.

"I think it's time to go back home, my husband. Where we can be a family again. Boys?"

"Yes'm," Forrest and Mark chorused, grinning from ear to ear.

Then Joby kissed Felicia, very tenderly, very softly on her bruised lips, and he touched her sand-strewn hair and stroked it gently. The breeze tugged at them and then died away as if the universe were holding its breath, restoring peace to the blood-soaked sands along the Brazos.